Frankie sprang backwards, startled.

A carving as tall as her brother Jin was staring at her. It had a square body and blocky hands and feet, as if it had been roughly hacked, in a hurry, from a lump of wood. It had jointed legs and arms, like a clumsy, life-size puppet, and it bristled all over with bits of sharp metal that had been hammered into its wooden body. Its head was free of metal, except for a crest of giant spikes that ran, like a Mohawk, over its smooth wooden skull, from its forehead to its spine.

'It's called Avenger,' said Mizz Z coolly. 'It once belonged to the Crocodile King . . .'

www.tamarindbooks.co.uk

*Also by S. P. Gates, and published by
Tamarind Books:*

ZILOMBO

THE CURSE OF THE

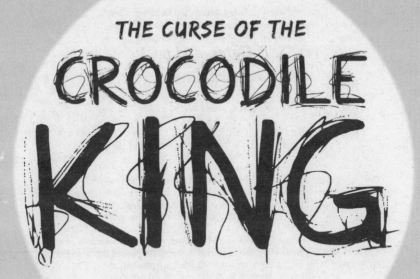

CROCODILE KING

S.P. GATES

Tamarind

THE CURSE OF THE CROCODILE KING
A TAMARIND BOOK 978 1 848 53052 2

First published in Great Britain by Tamarind Books,
an imprint of Random House Children's Books
A Random House Group Company

This edition published 2012

3 5 7 9 10 8 6 4 2

The Random House Group Limited supports the Forest Stewardship
Council (FSC®), the leading international forest certification organization.
Our books carrying the FSC label are printed on
FSC®-certified paper. FSC is the only forest certification
scheme endorsed by the leading environmental organizations,
including Greenpeace. Our paper procurement policy can be found at
www.randomhouse.co.uk/environment

MIX
Paper from
responsible sources
FSC® C016897

Set in 13/18pt Classic Garamond by
Falcon Oast Graphic Art Ltd.

Tamarind Books are published by Random House Children's Books,
61–63 Uxbridge Road, London W5 5SA

www.kidsatrandomhouse.co.uk
www.tamarindbooks.co.uk
www.randomhouse.co.uk

Addresses for companies within The Random House Group Limited can
be found at: www.randomhouse.co.uk/offices.htm

THE RANDOM HOUSE GROUP Limited Reg. No. 954009

A CIP catalogue record for this book is available from the British Library.

Printed and bound in Great Britain by
CPI Group (UK) Ltd, Croydon, CR0 4YY

THE CURSE OF THE CROCODILE KING

Previously . . .

Twenty years ago, in a lakeside village in Central Africa, a small crowd of people stood waiting by a baobab tree. The baobab tree was perhaps a thousand years old. It had once been twenty metres tall but, with age, most of it had crumbled away. Now it looked dead. All that was left was a big, hollow trunk that bulged like a potbelly. And a few bare, twiggy branches clutching the air like skeleton fingers.

The tree was an ancient relic. But in its trunk was a door that looked brand-new. This door was closed. A pink ribbon had been wound around the baobab and tied in a bow.

Among the crowd was a girl with a patch over one eye. She was slender and tall with a dignified air and a stubborn tilt to her chin. Beside her was Kapito, her little brother. Their dad, Mr P. C. Zauyamakanda, stood behind them.

'Here he comes!' someone shouted. Everyone stared down the road at the cloud of red dust approaching the village.

'Where's Grandma?' asked the tall girl with the eye patch, whose name was Miss A. J. Zauyamakanda.

'Grandma wouldn't come,' her dad answered. 'She says no one has any business messing with this old baobab. Especially opening it up. She says no good will come of it.'

'Why not?' asked his daughter. 'What's so special about this tree?'

'Gran can't exactly remember. She says some old king's mummified body was buried inside its hollow trunk. But that's all ancient history. He must have turned to dust centuries ago. If his body was ever put inside that tree in the first place. You know Gran and her old stories!'

'Did Gran say anything else about this king?'

Her dad shrugged. 'Nothing much. Except that he was known as the "Crocodile King".

And people around here were terrified of him.'

'But . . .' began his daughter. She wanted to know more about this Crocodile King. Firstly, because she was a very curious girl and interested in everything that was going on. And secondly because, only two years ago, an old story had saved her life and the lives of her dad, mum and brother.

Miss A. J. Zauyamakanda flinched as she thought about this, and her trembling hand stole up to her black eye patch. She still had nightmares about that terrible day when she had lost one of her eyes.[1]

But there wasn't time for any more questions because suddenly a long, black limo appeared from the dust cloud.

The car screeched to a stop beside the baobab. The driver leaped out and opened the back door. A businessman in a smart suit and shades climbed from the limo.

'Who's the guy in the suit?' whispered

[1] *See* Zilombo, *Mizz Z's first adventure with Jin and Frankie, to find out more.*

Kapito, who had no idea what was going on and would rather be playing football with his mates.

'He's Mr Ulili, a local boy made good,' hissed Dad. 'He went to the city and made his fortune. They say he's a millionaire.'

'Wow,' said Kapito, impressed. 'How'd he make all that money?'

'He started a bathroom company. But, shhh!' hushed Dad. 'Mr Ulili is speaking.'

'This is a happy moment for me,' Mr Ulili declared. 'For a long time I've wanted to give something back to my home village. And here it is. Your new uni-sex, luxury public convenience!' Mr Ulili's driver handed his boss a pair of scissors and the businessman snipped the pink ribbon. 'I declare this public toilet officially open!' he cried. Proudly he threw open the door to show the gleaming porcelain loo and hand-wash basin inside.

Kapito sniggered behind his hand.

Miss Zauyamakanda was also unimpressed. *All this fuss about a toilet!* she thought. *He could have given us something useful. Like a proper football pitch.*

Miss Zauyamakanda loved to play football. But their football pitch was a patch in the bush. When you fancied a kickabout, you had to clear it with machetes. And two days ago, the goalposts had been chewed to dust by termites.

Mr Ulili stopped talking. The crowd clapped politely. 'Thank you,' the village chief said, 'for your generous gift. It will be much appreciated by visitors to our village on market days.'

Mr Ulili consulted his watch. 'I'd like to stay for the celebrations,' he said, 'but I'm afraid I must rush back to the city.'

The driver started up the limo's engine.

'Before I leave,' said Mr Ulili, smiling, 'I'll be your new public toilet's very first customer.'

And he nipped inside the baobab and closed the door.

But suddenly, after only a few seconds, the

door in the ancient tree's trunk burst open. Mr Ulili came rushing out and stumbled towards the limo. His eyes were wide and staring. He was sweating as if in a fever, but his face was cold, ashy grey.

Mr Ulili wrenched open the limo door and tumbled into the passenger seat. 'Get me out of here!' he screamed in a panicky voice at his driver. 'Go, go, go!'

The crowd watched, bewildered, as the limo roared away at top speed, the passenger door still flapping open. They saw the red dust cloud it raised getting smaller and smaller. Then disappear altogether.

'What's wrong with that guy?' asked the chief. 'He looked terrified. As if he'd seen a ghost.'

'*Hmmm*, ghosts,' murmured Miss A. J. Zauyamakanda. 'That's interesting. I wonder if Gran knows anything more about this Crocodile King . . .'

After Mr Ulili had been scared out of his skin,

some people wouldn't set foot inside the new public convenience. They said it was haunted by the Croc King's spirit.

Others jeered, 'That's ridiculous. There's nothing to be scared of. It's a perfectly ordinary toilet.' To prove this, some of them even used it. But strangely, none of them ever used it twice.

'Did you *see* anything?' people would ask them when they stumbled out, grey-faced and shaking.

'No,' they'd answer, if they answered at all. 'I didn't see anything. I just felt *really* afraid. I had to get out of there!'

Then, one morning, when people came out of their houses, they found that someone had sneaked along in the night and nailed planks over the door in the baobab's trunk. Now no one could get into the public convenience. People in the village didn't seem to mind about this act of vandalism. In fact, they were secretly relieved.

'I wonder who did this?' said Mr

Zauyamakanda as he stared at the planks nailed over the door.

His daughter, standing by his side, said nothing at all.

So the years rolled by. Miss A. J. Zauyamakanda grew up and became Mizz Z. In her spare time she coached the Lakeside Queens, a girls' football team. But her main job was as Chief Inspector for RAAAA, a secret organization that inspected ancient artefacts – particularly those with dangerous, ancient powers.

Granny Zauyamakanda lived to be ninety-two. As she grew older her memory faded. She forgot all about the Crocodile King. And most people forgot, too, that there'd ever been a toilet inside the old baobab tree.

Chapter One

Twenty years after Mr Ulili opened his public loo in Africa, Jin Aaron Sparks, a British-born half-Chinese boy, sat in a burger bar in the North of England. He was with his dad and his big sister Frankie.

Frankie looked like an evil fairy, in a party frock she'd found in a charity shop. It had been pink when she'd bought it, with frills and sequins. But Frankie had dyed it funeral black, then completed her outfit with thick black tights and biker boots.

Frankie liked to be rebellious and different. She didn't mind people staring. But Jin was just the opposite – he hated attracting attention. The more he could blend in, the more he liked it.

Frankie put down her cheeseburger. 'Can I get a tattoo?' she asked her dad.

'No,' said Dad, a slow-moving, slow-talking guy who looked like a big, shambling bear.

'But *you've* got tattoos,' Frankie pointed out.

Dad had tattoos on the knuckles of both hands. They had faded now to blue blurs. Mum had told Jin they were from Dad's wild biker days and that they'd once said, 'LOVE' and 'HATE'.

'That doesn't mean you can get one,' Dad told Frankie.

'So it's, like, do as I say, not as I do?' said Frankie scornfully.

A cunning glint came into Dad's eyes. He said, 'Oh, I don't care! Just go out and get one. In fact, I approve. OK? I *want* you to get a tattoo. I'd be really upset if you didn't.'

Instead of saying, 'I don't want one now,' like Dad expected, Frankie gave a triumphant hoot of laughter. 'Ha-ha! You just gave me permission. Thanks!' She grinned at Jin. 'Parents,' she said. 'They're *sooo* predictable.' And then she stomped off to find some more ketchup, her party frock puffed up around her like a black storm cloud.

Jin grinned too. Frankie liked winding people up. Sometimes she drove Mum and Dad round the bend. But Jin mostly got on all right with his big sister.

'I wish Mum was back,' his dad sighed. 'She can handle Frankie better than I can.'

'No one can handle Frankie.' Jin chortled. 'Except maybe Mizz Z.'

As Jin said that, a picture flashed into his mind. It was of the formidable Mizz Z – a tall, majestic woman with one fierce amber eye and an eye patch on the other that made her look part pirate captain, part warrior queen. During Mizz Z's last mission, when they'd teamed up to fight the monster Zilombo, Jin and Frankie had learned new respect for each other.

'But Mizz Z's not here, is she?' Dad

pointed out. 'She flew to Africa a month ago. Who knows when she's coming back?'

But Mum would *definitely* be home next week. She was in Hong Kong with Smiler, their baby brother, showing him off to the aunties and other relatives. Grandma and Grandad Tang had gone with her. Jin had begged, 'Can't I come?' But Mum was strict about his education. She'd said, 'Not this time, you'd miss too much school.'

Dad took a fistful of French fries and stuffed them into his mouth. Then he opened up his laptop. 'Right,' he said, still chewing. 'Time for our video chat.'

Every day they had to link up with Mum so she could check how they were – and that Jin's face was healing.

The day before Mum left, Jin had opened a cupboard door and somehow smashed it into his nose. It had hurt like crazy; he'd danced around, cursing. He still had a plaster on it now: one with a skull on that made him look tough and sinister. Jin often had a plaster stuck on somewhere. He had clumsy child syndrome. 'The *proper* name for it is dyspraxia,' Jin would say helpfully, if anyone asked.

If they wanted to know, 'What's that actually mean?' he'd answer, 'It means my co-ordination's a bit rubbish.' Then he'd always add, shrugging, 'It's no big deal.'

And it wasn't, most of the time. As long as Jin wasn't rushed, he could avoid accidents. And do the things he found difficult like, for example, tying shoelaces, catching a ball, telling right from left . . .

'Here we go,' said Dad.

His big hands, with those faded tattoos, paused over the computer just as Frankie plonked herself back in her seat with a fistful of ketchup sachets.

'Remind me. How do I do this again?' Dad frowned.

'Dad!' exclaimed Frankie. 'I've told you loads of times.' She slid the laptop towards her, stroked the touch pad with nimble fingers, tapped a few keys with her black-painted nails. Then slid it back.

'It's Mum!' said Dad, amazed like he always was, as if it was magic. Frankie and Jin exchanged pitying looks.

Jin stood behind Dad so he could see the screen. 'Hey, Mum,' he said. 'I'm fine. We're all fine. My nose is fine. It doesn't hurt any more.'

'What's that in the background? You're not in a burger bar, are you?' said Mum suspiciously.

'A burger bar?' said Jin, moving to block Mum's view. 'No, course not, Mum. Dad's been cooking us tea every night.'

'Jin, you're the worst liar ever,' whispered Frankie.

'*Shhh*, she'll hear,' hissed Dad out of the side of his mouth.

Quickly Jin changed the subject. 'Mum, I need a new phone. Bet you can get really cool ones in Hong Kong.'

'What, *another* phone?' said Mum.

'It's not my fault,' said Jin. 'I'm dyspraxic, aren't I?' He put a woeful expression on his face, but he was secretly smiling inside. Being accident prone was often a pain. But there was one thing it was good for – at least people couldn't blame you for breaking things.

'So what actually happened to your old phone?' said Mum.

Jin leaned over Dad's shoulder and spun the laptop round to face Frankie before he had to confess he'd left his phone on a bus.

Frankie said, 'Hi, Mum! I'm doing a shift at the Money Tree tonight.'

The Money Tree bakery was in Chinatown. Four nights a week, from seven o'clock until nine, Frankie worked there to earn extra pocket money. It was owned by Mr and Mrs Tang, their uncle and auntie.

Frankie said, 'Bye, Mum!' She slid the laptop back to Dad.

He only had time for a few quick words before his mobile started beeping.

'Got to go, sweetheart!' he told Mum. 'My

work phone's ringing.' Dad was on emergency call-out. He was a rodent control technician for the council.

Any time Dad talked about his job, Frankie would yawn and roll her eyes. 'Look, Dad,' she'd tell him. 'Just face facts. You're a rat-catcher. Right? Don't even try to make it interesting.' In her opinion it was a dumb job. And really, really uncool.

Sometimes Dad insisted, 'You've got to be smart to catch a rat.'

But Frankie always thought, *Are you joking? Granny Tang's cat is really stupid. And he does it all the time.*

Dad listened to his caller for a long time. Whoever was on the phone sounded really upset. Dad tried to calm them down.

'It's OK,' he reassured them in his slow, steady voice. 'Don't worry. I'll deal with it.'

Behind their father's back, Frankie and Jin, sick of waiting, pretended to hang themselves.

'I'll be there right away,' said Dad, finally ending the call.

'Rat-catcher to the rescue!' mocked Frankie.

'So what was that all about? You were on the phone for ages,' grumbled Jin.

'You know the City Museum?' said Dad.

Jin nodded. The museum was right at the back of the Money Tree bakery, on the other side of the old city wall.

'That was their new director on the phone. They've got a rat in one of their toilets.'

'In a toilet?' said Jin. 'Gross.'

Dad gave a casual shrug. 'It's quite common. Part of my job. Rats often come up in toilets, paddle about in the bowl.'

'Too much information, Dad,' Frankie protested.

But Dad seemed eager to tell them. He even sounded quite excited. 'The rat's in some kind of special toilet – their newest exhibit. A toilet in a *tree*, apparently, that's just arrived from Africa.'

'In a tree? From Africa?' said Jin, curious despite himself. 'Are you sure?'

'I might have misheard that bit,' admitted Dad. 'Some people go nuts when they see rats. It's hard to understand what they're saying.'

'So what else did this director guy tell you?' asked Jin.

'He said there were *planks* nailed over the toilet door,' said Dad. 'Don't ask me why. Anyway, he levered them off, opened the door a bit, saw the rat inside and slammed it shut. And he hasn't opened the door since. We'd better get going, find out what it's all about.'

'What do you mean, *we*?' said Jin.

'You've got to come too,' said Dad. 'Frankie's off to the bakery. And you're not staying home alone. Your mum would go mental.'

'Dad, I'm not a little kid any more!' protested Jin.

But Dad was already striding from the burger bar.

'Ha-ha,' Frankie teased Jin. 'Have a great time, bro'. Wish I was coming with you.'

'I got other things to d...' growled Jin, plodding after Dad, ... thunder.

Outside Frankie said, 'See you later.'

'We can give you a lift,' said Dad. 'We can drop you right outside the bakery.'

Frankie looked at Dad's big council van painted bright canary-yellow, with PEST CONTROL on each side in giant, unmissable letters. Dad had the uncoolest job. And the uncoolest vehicle to go with it.

'It's OK,' she said. 'I'll walk.'

Ji... ...otest all the way to the City Museu... ...e couldn't keep it up; he was a naturally chatty person. By the time they pulled into the museum car park, he was talking again.

'There aren't many other cars here,' he said, gazing around, surprised at all the empty spaces.

'That's because it's past six o'clock,' said Dad. 'The museum is closed for the day.' Then he asked Jin, 'Have you ever been in this place?'

'Yeah, once, on a school trip,' said Jin, yawning hugely at the memory. 'It was dead boring.'

The museum was in the old part of the city,

where there were cobbled streets, crooked buildings crammed together, and the ruins of a massive wall that had once surrounded the city in medieval times. On the other side of the wall was Chinatown. Jin could smell fragrant smells drifting over from the Money Tree bakery.

Mmmm, thought Jin, his mouth watering. He could have been at the bakery in ten seconds. All he needed to do was dash through the Friendship Arch that had been built in a gap in the old city wall. The Friendship Arch was a fabulous gold and red structure twelve metres high, the gateway to Chinatown. At the top it had seven pagoda-style roofs and two hundred and eighty-three painted dragons. More dragons, said people proudly, than the arch in Liverpool. *Mmmm*, thought Jin again, his nose twitching as it picked up another delicious scent. *Egg tarts – my favourite.*

But this was no time to think of cakes. Dad was tooling up, as if he was going to war. He'd thrown open the back of his bright yellow council van and climbed into his rat-fighting trousers. They were tight around the ankles so no rats could run up inside them. Now he was strapping on a leather belt, hung with all sorts of rat-trapping equipment. Then he pulled on his big leather gauntlets to protect him from bites.

'It's me versus the vermin,' said Dad grimly. 'And I never underestimate the enemy. Rats are very smart animals.'

'Oh, yeah?' said Jin doubtfully.

He had never been with Dad before on a rat-hunting mission. Jin wasn't as sneery about Dad's job as Frankie; it was just that he'd never taken the slightest interest in it. So he was surprised to see how Dad seemed to become another person as he loaded up with gear, cages to trap rats in and bait to entice them.

It's like, all of a sudden, he's an action man, thought Jin, astonished.

Dad's sleepy look disappeared. His eyes became sharp and flinty. Even his walk and voice changed. They became brisk and purposeful. 'Come on,' he snapped at Jin urgently. 'We've got a job to do.' And he went striding off like a soldier across the car park.

'Hey, wait for me!' said Jin, caught off guard by Dad's speed.

He went lurching after Dad and immediately tripped over a manhole cover. He fell sprawling to the ground. But he leaped up again, as if it hadn't happened. Jin never let little setbacks like this deter him. For him, they were just a normal part of everyday life.

When Jin caught up, his dad was round the side of the museum, at a little door marked PRIVATE.

'This is where the guy on the phone said to knock,' Dad explained. 'He said the main doors would be locked.'

A sudden thought struck Jin. 'This rat,' he said. 'You're going to kill it after you've caught it, aren't you?'

Jin already knew this was part of Dad's job.

But he'd always pushed it to the back of his mind. Until now.

'Has to be done, I'm afraid,' was Dad's answer.

Jin shuddered. It wasn't that he loved rats, or anything, but he didn't like the idea of them being killed.

'I don't have to watch, do I?' he said.

'Of course not,' said Dad. 'I don't *like* doing it. But at least I do it humanely, so they don't suffer. I take pride in that. Otherwise people drown them, or bash their brains out with broom handles. Now *that's* really cruel.'

Jin stared. He'd never heard Dad talk about pride before. It was all a bit unsettling.

But Jin's brain had no time to deal with that now, because Dad was knocking loudly. After a while, the little door creaked open. Two eyes, cold and green as glass marbles, peered round it. 'I'm the rodent control technician you sent for,' said Dad. 'I've come about the rat in the toilet.'

The eyes narrowed suspiciously. 'I don't know about any rat in a toilet,' said a voice even more unfriendly than the eyes. 'No one tells me anything around here.'

'I was told the toilet is in a *tree*?' said Dad. 'But I might not have heard that right.'

'Ah, yes,' said the voice with fussy precision. 'I believe the *tree* you are referring to is in fact a baobab, commonly known as a "dead rat tree" because it has large, fur-covered seeds that dangle from the branches on long stalks, similar to rats' tails.'

'A dead rat tree!' murmured Dad to Jin, grinning. 'That's my kinda tree!' Then he demanded, 'Are you going to let us in?' He was all fired up to get on with the job.

Jin still couldn't get his head around the change in his father. He was so dynamic! So different from the laid-back, dozy dad he was at home who always said, 'Go ask Mum,' if you wanted him to make a decision.

The museum door opened wide, revealing a wizened old guy wearing a fusty suit with a waistcoat and bow tie. His beard and hair were grey and dry and brittle as straw, and his skin was grey too. He looked like he'd crumble to dust, like an Egyptian mummy, if he went out in strong sunlight.

Dad stormed in with Jin behind him. 'Where's the rat?' he demanded.

'Oh, that's nothing to do with me,' said the guy who'd let them in. 'Not my department at all. I'm Doctor Cramp, the curator of Ancient Artefacts.'

Jin was instantly reminded again of Mizz Z. It was her job to check that ancient artefacts, especially dangerous ones, were kept in safe conditions and could never regain their old powers.

'I've got a friend who inspects artefacts,' he blurted out. 'You know, statues, masks, shields, ancient stuff like that. Do you know her? She's called Mizz Z. She's Chief Inspector for RAAAA. That's the Risk Assessment Agency for Ancient Artefacts. Their inspectors work undercover all over the world.'

'I have never heard of her, or that organiz-ation,' said Dr Cramp sniffily.

'Well, you won't have, it's secret . . .' Jin started to explain, before thinking, *Doh! I shouldn't have told him.*

But the curator's chilly eyes had already turned away.

'Our new director must have called you,' he told Dad. When he said the word *director*, Jin saw Dr Cramp's lip curl with scorn. 'But the director's in a meeting at the moment,' he continued, 'discussing how to *modernize* the museum, make it more *popular* with visitors.'

'No problem,' said Dad. 'Just direct me to this toilet.'

'That way,' said the curator, vaguely waving his arm. 'You'll find the toilet in the inter-active, child-friendly, fun part of the museum.'

Dr Cramp spat out the words *interactive*, *child-friendly* and *fun* as if they disgusted him. He seemed like a frail old guy but suddenly his eyes blazed with such bitter rage that Jin's heart leaped with alarm.

'Of course, the new director didn't consult me about these changes,' hissed Dr Cramp. 'I've been here for fifty years, studying Central African artefacts. Then this ignorant young man comes along and actually *removes* my artefacts from their display cases. He says they are stuffy and of no interest to modern children! He even says I'm too old to do my job. That it's time I retired! Well, I can assure you that is not going to happen!' The curator gave Jin a venomous glare as if it was all his fault, then slid away. 'Let yourselves out when you want to leave,' rasped his voice from the shadows. Then there was silence.

'*Phew!*' gasped Jin. 'Has he gone? Don't think he likes kids much. And he *hates* that new director guy, doesn't he?'

But Dad didn't answer. His mind was focused again on rat-fighting. He hoisted up his belt of weaponry and marched off.

Jin hurried to catch up with him. This was the bit of the museum he remembered from the school trip: a warren of dark corridors which led to vast gloomy halls crammed with dusty exhibits in glass cases. But he didn't remember the place *feeling* like this.

Jin might have a problem with balance and co-ordination. He might, sometimes, have to force his disobedient limbs to behave. But he had one huge talent. He was ace at sensing tiny changes in mood and atmosphere – both in people and places. He could read faces like a book, sense when a place felt safe or threatening. Because when you're dyspraxic and can't run away fast from danger, being extra-alert to things like that is your best protection.

And in the museum Jin felt something disturbing. He could practically taste it in the air. A sense of menace. As if something frightful was lurking somewhere, just waiting to be released.

'Dad,' whispered Jin, when he caught up. 'Can you, like, feel anything *weird*?'

Jin regretted the question as soon as he'd asked it. He should have known better. He'd learned long ago that most other people didn't notice things like he did. But Dad stopped and listened. Then he raised his head, almost seeming to sniff the air.

He said, 'You're right, son. Let's get this job done and get out of here. There's something definitely creepy about this place.'

Jin was really surprised that Dad had felt it too. He didn't know whether to feel scared or reassured. 'Dad,' he whispered, 'are the hairs on the back of your neck twitching?'

'Yes,' said Dad. 'They are.'

But suddenly Jin forgot about that feeling of dread, because they'd arrived at some big double doors. A sign above them said: TOILETS OF THE WORLD.

'It's *got* to be in here,' said Dad. 'Come on.' And he strode through with Jin following.

Jin murmured, '*Wow.*' The big hall was bright and welcoming. It had been painted in cheerful colours, and all the dusty old display cabinets had been cleared away. In their place was a toilet exhibition, with loos – ancient and modern – from all over the globe.

He started to walk around. There was a golden toilet from the tomb of a pharaoh. *Put in the pyramid with him*, the sign next to it said, *so he could use it in the afterlife*. There was a hi-tech Japanese karaoke loo that played tunes you could sing along to. There was a toilet from ancient Rome, with twenty seats so people could chat to each other and exchange the latest gossip.

'Hey,' Jin told Dad, 'this is definitely more interesting than when I was here before.'

But Dad said, 'This is no time to look at toilets. Can you see a tree anywhere?'

Jin peered into a little side room: 'There's a tree in here. Come and look.'

The tree had a hollow trunk about as high as a telephone box but bottle-shaped. A few shrivelled, twiggy branches sprouted out of its narrow top. Below that, in the swollen part of the trunk, was a door.

'That must be it,' said Dad, leading the way

into the side room. 'Looks like it died a long time ago. Most of its branches are missing.'

As soon as Jin followed Dad in, he could sense it. That feeling of menace came flooding back. But there was something else – a sort of pressure building, a kind of unbearable tension. As if something very big and powerful was about to burst out of its cage. Jin even glanced fearfully over his shoulder. But there was nothing in the room except him, Dad and an old, dead-looking baobab tree.

Surely Dad felt it too?

But Dad's mind was on the job. He was busy baiting cage traps with a rat's favourite snack: peanut butter.

Jin tried to distract his brain too. He started reading the sign on the tree that told you all about it.

Our new exhibit, the sign said, *has been kindly donated to the City Museum by an unknown benefactor. This ancient tree has been brought all the way from a village in Central Africa. A toilet in a hollow tree may seem strange, but throughout history baobabs have been used as prisons, chapels, stables, public conveniences, and even burial places for chiefs and kings—*

'Right,' Dad told Jin, interrupting his reading. 'I'm opening the toilet door. You ready?'

'Yes,' said Jin, wishing he had a pair of rat-catching pants like Dad's.

'It'll either go in the traps, or run like mad. And don't you try to catch it. Rats can bite through steel. You just stand still. Leave the rat to me.'

Dad opened the door just a fraction. Instantly a massive rat, far too big to fit in the traps, hurled itself out, straight at Dad's throat.

'Dad!' yelled Jin, ignoring his father's orders to stand still. He rushed forward to help rip the furry beast off Dad's neck.

'It's OK, it's OK.' Dad held up a hand to stop Jin crashing into him.

Jin backed off, bewildered, his heart

thumping. He couldn't believe what he saw. Wasn't Dad a rat's worst enemy? So why was he cuddling this one, cradling its quivering body in his arms, as if to comfort it?

'Dad!' said Jin. 'What are you doing? That rat just attacked you.'

'It didn't,' said Dad, still hugging the rodent. 'It was just desperate to get out of that tree. Something scared it almost to death in there.'

Jin still didn't understand. 'I thought you *killed* rats.'

'That's my job,' said Dad. 'But the kind you get in this city are vermin. They live in the sewers and spread deadly diseases. This is a totally different species. It's an African Giant Pouched Rat – they live in burrows like rabbits and carry food in their cheek pouches like hamsters. They're really cute. Want to hold it?'

He handed over the huge, big-eared rat and Jin took it awkwardly.

'It's OK, it won't bite,' Dad said.

Jin stroked its fur. It was as big as a bunny but it looked like a giant hamster, brown all over with a white throat and belly, except where, on its white throat, there was a furry brown patch shaped like a star.

'What's it eat?' asked Jin.

Dad, of course, knew the answer. 'Mangoes and groundnuts and maize grains, stuff like that.'

'Is there *anything* you don't know about rats?' said Jin, impressed.

'Not much,' Dad admitted.

'You're a soppy old thing, aren't you?' said Jin to the rat as it snuggled against his jacket. 'Can we keep him, Dad? Can we? Frankie won't mind.'

Jin knew Mum would go mental. But he tried not to think about that. Mum wasn't here at the moment, was she? She was far away, in Hong Kong.

Dad didn't seem to hear Jin's question. He was too busy puzzling something out.

'That rat must have come in that tree all the

way from Africa,' he said. 'But how'd it get in there in the first place? Especially when the door was nailed shut.'

'Don't ask me,' shrugged Jin.

Only the Giant Pouched Rat knew the answer to that. In Africa it had been bumbling along, minding its own business, its fat cheeks stuffed with food, when an eagle had swooped down and grabbed it. Flying over the baobab with the rat in its claws, the eagle had dropped it by accident. The rat had plunged downwards, somehow slid through the thicket of branches that formed the toilet roof, and landed on the floor inside. It had thought this was its lucky day because it had escaped being an eagle's dinner. But then the poor creature had discovered that the walls were too slippery for it to climb out – and it was trapped inside the baobab with something so dreadful that its ratty heart almost stopped beating with fright.

'It seems very tame,' said Dad, 'and used to people.'

Safe in Jin's arms, the rat had finally stopped shuddering with fear. 'Don't worry,' Jin crooned, stroking its fur. 'I'll look after you. Bet you're missing Africa, aren't you? I'll get you a mango from Mr Ma's grocery.'

But the rat must have sensed it again – that same terror it had felt inside its baobab prison. The terror seemed to be creeping out of the open toilet door, spreading like poison gas throughout the room.

'What's happening?' said Jin, feeling his throat tighten. 'I can't breathe.'

Suddenly the rat took off. It leaped out of Jin's arms and ran skittering across the tiled floor.

'He's escaped!' cried Jin.

'Quick, close the door to the toilet,' said Dad, 'so it can't get back inside.'

But the baobab was the last place the rat wanted to go. It ran out of the small room and disappeared into the 'Toilets of the World' exhibition.

'We've got to find him!' raved Jin. 'I just told him I'd look after him!'

He felt personally responsible now. He raced out into the main hall, frantically looking around.

Dad followed, cursing under his breath. 'I thought this would be a routine job. But it's getting more complicated by the minute. We could be here all night.'

'I don't care, I'm not leaving without him,' said Jin. 'Come on, Dad, help me look.'

Chapter Three

Frankie was almost at the Money Tree bakery. She passed the red wooden pillars of the Friendship Arch. Through the arch she could see Dad's yellow van parked in the City Museum car park.

Frankie smiled. She loved the narrow main street of Chinatown at night. It was so lively and bustling. She loved the bright neon signs everywhere that sparkled pink, orange and blue. And the six big tasselled lanterns outside the Ocean Bull, which glowed deep crimson.

'Hi, Auntie!' she called out.

Frankie seemed to be talking to her boots. But, in fact, she was shouting through a grille in the pavement. Steam came up through it, along with the spicy scent of freshly baked buns.

Hmmm, thought Frankie. *Curry Beef Puffs.* She could see Auntie through the grille – down there in the huge cellar kitchen of the bakery, fussing over the Iron Dragon. The Iron Dragon was an ancient bun-steaming stove. All the other equipment in the bakery was modern, made of gleaming stainless steel. Only the Iron Dragon was a relic from a bygone age.

Auntie, in her snowy-white baker's overall and cap, peered up through the grille. She wiped her forehead.

Frankie knelt on the pavement, her black skirts spreading around her like crows' wings. 'Is the Iron Dragon causing trouble today?' she yelled down.

Auntie nodded ruefully. But it was no surprise – the old beast was always causing trouble.

Near the grille, just outside the shop door, growing in a big blue and white pot, was the money tree that had given the bakery its name. It was ancient, with a thick, plaited trunk, and it had seven frondy leaves on each slender branch instead of the usual five. That made it especially lucky, like finding a four-leaved clover.

Auntie and Uncle often said modestly, 'We owe our success to that old money tree.'

But everyone knew it wasn't really down to the money tree. It was because they were such great bakers, canny business folk and all-round nice people. Frankie liked them a lot.

Frankie was about to go through the bakery door when it crashed open and Mr Lu and Uncle came spilling out into the street, arguing with each other in Mandarin. Mr Lu was from the rival bakery down the street. He had a very hot temper. Still yelling, he went back to his own bakery, The Lotus Flower.

'What was all that about?' asked Frankie, who understood a bit of Mandarin but got lost if people talked too fast.

'That man!' said Uncle in English. He was trembling with anger. 'He says that we shouldn't be advertising our Char Sui buns as buns. He says they aren't buns at all but dumplings. How dare he say I don't know the difference between a bun and a dumpling!'

'What a cheek!' agreed Frankie, as outraged as Uncle. 'I'm going to go down there and make him apologize!'

'No, no, Frankie,' begged Uncle who, although he felt insulted, didn't want this to become a full-scale war. 'That will only make things worse.'

'Huh!' said Frankie, unconvinced. 'He's just jealous because you won that prize.'

The Money Tree had been voted the city's best bakery. It was *the* cool place to go and eat custard tarts and drink bubbly tea.

'*Everyone* hangs out at the Money Tree,' said Frankie. '*No one* goes to Mr Lu's.'

Then they both forgot about Mr Lu. Because an anguished cry drifted up through the grille, followed by black smoke and a smell of burning.

'That's Auntie!' Frankie cried.

'The Iron Dragon is being a pig today,' explained Uncle. 'It's driving us crazy.' And with a worried frown on his face he hurried off into the bakery and down the stone steps to the cellar kitchen.

Frankie pushed open the bakery door, put on her white overall and stood behind the counter. She tried to text one of her friends. 'You forgot to charge your phone up!' she raged at herself. Busy fiddling with her phone, she didn't notice the customer waiting for attention.

The customer coughed apologetically. '*Ahem.*'

'Yes!' snapped Frankie.

'*Er,*' said the customer, shrivelling under her fierce gaze. 'Could you tell me, please? Those buns there that are labelled "pineapple buns", do they have pineapple inside?'

'Of course not!' said Frankie scornfully, as if it was a really stupid question. 'They just *look* like pineapples. They don't actually *taste* like them.'

'Oh, right,' said the customer. He scurried off. Frankie thought, *Good. That's got rid of him.*

But Auntie had been at the top of the stairs, listening. She came charging into the bakery. She looked hot and flustered and her face was covered with black smuts.

'How dare you!' she yelled at her niece. 'How dare you speak to one of our customers with rudeness! Here at the Money Tree we pride ourselves on our polite and friendly service!'

Frankie stared at Auntie, amazed – her aunt had never before shouted at her or told her off. It was on the tip of Frankie's tongue to answer back but she could see that, today, Auntie's nerves were in shreds. The Iron Dragon, that metal tyrant that ruled the Tangs' basement kitchen, had clearly driven her close to breaking point.

A big fat tear rolled down Auntie's cheek. She wiped it away and smeared her cheek with soot. 'I'm so tired,' she said. 'The Iron Dragon keeps going out. And when we get it re-lit, it sends out clouds of black smoke. Then it gets too hot and burns the buns. I think it just likes being awkward.'

The last of Frankie's aggression melted away. Instead, she just felt desperately sorry for Auntie. 'You're slaves to that horrible thing,' she told her. 'You ought to get rid of it. Sell it for scrap.'

'Shhh!' warned Auntie, as if the Iron Dragon could hear them talking about it. Then she whispered: 'You know I can't do that. I wish I could.'

'But it rules your lives!' protested Frankie.

Auntie gave a weary sigh. 'I know. But we just have to put up with it. We've got no choice.'

'Well, you don't have to worry about me,' Frankie assured her. 'I'm sorry I was rude to that customer. I promise to be dead polite from now on.'

Auntie's face brightened. 'You're a lovely, kind girl, Frankie. And a big help to Uncle and me.' Then, putting on a brave smile, she scuttled back down to the kitchen.

Lovely and kind? thought Frankie, surprised. And a big help? *I never knew that.* It surprised her too that it felt secretly good to be called *lovely* and *kind.* As long as it was only by Auntie – and none of her mates at school found out.

For the rest of her shift, Frankie faithfully kept her promise. She smiled at customers until her jaw ached. She was patient when people who'd never been to a Chinese bakery before asked, 'Exactly what is *inside* a moon cake?' And she even tried out her shaky Mandarin when the great-great-granny from Mr Ma's grocery, who was one hundred years old, came shuffling in with her ivory walking cane.

It was one minute to nine and Frankie was about to close up when the shop bell tinkled.

Oh, no, not more customers, she thought. *I'm fed up of being friendly.*

A tall woman with an eye patch came striding in. She wore a headwrap and dress in sizzling colours: hot pink, flaming orange, scorching yellow. She lit up the Money Tree bakery like a firework display.

'Hello, Frankie,' she said.

'Mizz Z!' Frankie gasped. 'You've come back!'

Chapter Four

Frankie flipped the sign over from OPEN to CLOSED and locked the bakery door. Then she went back to the counter, where Mizz Z was perched on a high stool, still managing to look graceful and dignified.

'I meant to come back to your city sooner,' explained Mizz Z. 'But I was delayed by the ancient statue of a winged lion in Indonesia. It rather inconveniently escaped.'

Frankie hated showing surprise – it wasn't cool. But you just couldn't help it with Mizz Z. She often casually let slip the most mind-boggling facts.

'You mean, it came to life and just flew away?' she said, her eyes widening.

Mizz Z gave a brisk nod. 'That's about it.'

'Was it very dangerous?' asked Frankie.

'Need you ask?' said Mizz Z. 'They wouldn't have sent for *me*, otherwise. Some *junior* inspector could have dealt with it.'

'But how did you get this winged lion back?' asked Frankie. 'What did you do? Shoot it down or something? Catch it in a net?'

'I cannot say anything more on the subject,' said Mizz Z, clamping her lips firmly shut.

'Is that because the mission was top secret?' asked Frankie.

'Of course,' said Mizz Z. 'As you well know, most of my missions for RAAAA are secret and undercover. So, shall we talk about something else? Like how you are doing at school. What are your grades, for instance?'

Frankie sighed. Sometimes the contradictory Mizz Z made you gasp in wonder. But sometimes she could be just like Mum. Ducking the question about grades, Frankie blurted out, 'It's really great to see you again.'

Mizz Z's stern, hawk-like features softened

for a moment into a warm, friendly smile. 'And it's good to see you too, Frankie,' she said. Then she got back to business. In her crisp Chief Inspector's voice she explained, 'It's time for my annual inspection of some ancient artefacts in your City Museum.'

'That's just near here,' said Frankie. 'On the other side of the wall.'

'Yes, I know that,' said Mizz Z with an impatient flash of her amber eye. 'I have been there before. Usually it is very straightforward. The artefacts are on display, always in the same place. So I pretend I am just an *ordinary* person, a visitor to the museum. I go in, check there is no risk, and leave. Job done. And they never know the Chief Inspector of RAAAA has been. Well, this time there has been a tiny glitch. I went there this afternoon—'

'Actually,' interrupted Frankie, 'Jin and Dad are in the museum now.'

'Really,' said Mizz Z. 'Why is that?'

But before Frankie had time to tell her, a voice from the basement called, 'Frankie, have you locked up?' And Auntie trudged up from the kitchen.

She did a double-take when she saw the majestic Mizz Z sitting on a bakery stool. Frankie quickly explained. 'Auntie, this is Mizz Z. You remember, we told you about her.'

'Oh, yes,' said Auntie. 'I heard all about that dreadful Zilombo – how it kidnapped Smiler and climbed with him up to the metro bridge. You went after that monster and saved Smiler's life!'

'Only with the help of Frankie and Jin,' Mizz Z pointed out.

But Auntie was already making a low, respectful bow. Mizz Z rose from her stool, her bronze arm bracelets clinking, and made one in return. And then spoke to Auntie in fluent Mandarin.

After some more polite talk between them that Frankie couldn't follow, Auntie took the money from the till, bowed again to Mizz Z and disappeared.

'What did you and Auntie say to each other?' Frankie asked Mizz Z.

'Dear me,' said Mizz Z disapprovingly, 'did you not understand? You really should improve your Mandarin. She said that she and your uncle are going home now. But we can stay here and chat. So long as you lock up again when we leave.'

But Frankie knew Mizz Z didn't like idle chat, especially when she was on a mission. 'What happened in the City Museum this afternoon?' she asked her.

'As I was saying, the artefacts weren't in their usual display case,' said Mizz Z. 'They must have been stored away down in the cellar. This makes my inspection a bit more tricky. It means I must get into the cellar store rooms somehow and find them.'

'I know how to get into the museum cellar,' said Frankie.

It was Mizz Z's turn to look surprised. She did this by lifting, very slightly, the eyebrow over her one good eye. 'You are a resourceful girl, I must say,' she told Frankie. 'You remind me of me when I was your age.'

Frankie felt a warm glow inside. It was the highest praise Mizz Z could have given her. Encouraged, she said, 'The museum is practically at the back of the bakery. There's only the city wall between them. But their cellars connect *under* the wall.'

'How convenient,' said Mizz Z. 'Do your auntie and uncle know about this underground link between the two buildings?'

'No, only me,' said Frankie with a hint of pride.

Frankie knew this city better than anyone. She liked prowling around its secret, neglected corners, its weedy wastelands, its high and low places. And everywhere she explored, she spray-painted her personal tag – a tiny red Chinese dragon. As if to say, 'Frankie was here.'

'Lead me to the museum, then,' said Mizz Z. She followed Frankie down the steps to the cellar kitchen. 'Good heavens,' she said, staring upwards.

The Iron Dragon was in the centre of the kitchen, towering over even Mizz Z, reaching almost to the cellar ceiling. It was rearing up on mighty clawed feet. Its snaky body was covered in black, iron scales and its fierce head, half dragon, half lion, had horns, a flowing beard and two bulging eyes. Steam hissed from its flaring nostrils. Behind its back curled a crested tail that ended in a spear-like tip.

'It's Auntie and Uncle's old bun-steaming stove,' explained Frankie, hardly giving it a glance.

'It is not any old bun-steaming stove,' corrected Mizz Z, still staring. 'I can't be one hundred per cent certain. Not until I have done some checks. But it looks to me like the legendary Iron Dragon.'

'You know its name!' marvelled Frankie. She shouldn't really have been surprised. Mizz Z seemed to know about everything.

'The old stories mention an ancient stove like this,' explained Mizz Z. 'But even we at

RAAAA had no idea it really existed. How intriguing,' she said, going closer to inspect the metal monster. 'How long has it been down here?'

'Oh, ages,' said Frankie. 'It came in bits from China. It was a gift to Uncle's grandad from one of his relatives. It's been here ever since the bakery opened.'

Mizz Z went closer to inspect the metal monster. 'Fascinating,' she murmured. There were three huge iron doors in its metal belly, one above the other. The bottom one was the furnace.

'Careful,' said Frankie as Mizz Z went closer. 'It's *very* hot. They keep it lit all the time. It's a nightmare if it goes out.'

Above the furnace door, which glowed red around its edges, was the door to the water tank, which heated up and made the steam that rose to cook the buns above. But there were no buns cooking now. The oven door was wide-open, showing racks of empty shelves.

'You ought to see it when it's going full blast,' said Frankie. 'It's like it's alive. Flames come out its mouth. It makes roaring, hissing sounds like a real dragon.'

'It's a magnificent beast,' said Mizz Z.

But Frankie disagreed. 'It's a *monster*. It's really hard work shovelling in coal, keeping the water tank topped up. Auntie has to climb up a stepladder to get the buns out! She wants to get rid of it, get a modern stove. But Uncle won't. When his grandad was dying, he made Uncle swear a solemn vow. Uncle had to promise he'd always use the Iron Dragon. Until it breaks down completely, of course. Then they can buy a new one.'

'*Aha*,' said Mizz Z. 'If I know my ancient artefacts, I bet it never does break down completely. It looks indestructible to me and I bet it will last for ever.'

'That's what Auntie's afraid of,' said Frankie.

'Well, what a find,' said Mizz Z, sounding pleased. 'I must report this to RAAAA, they will be very excited. But I have a job to do first. How do we get into the museum cellar from here?'

'This way,' said Frankie.

Beyond the kitchen, the cellar of the Money Tree bakery was like a rabbit warren. Switching on lights as she went, Frankie led Mizz Z through two tiny cell-like rooms full of bun-making ingredients, then along a narrow, brick-lined passage. In a third room she knelt down.

'This grille comes out,' she said,

Mizz Z knelt down too and helped Frankie heave the rusty metal out of the wall. It left a hole big enough to crawl through.

'Come on,' said Frankie, scooting forward on her hands and knees, the frills on her black dress trailing behind her like tentacles. 'Just through here and we're in the museum.'

Mizz Z followed in a more dignified manner. She dragged the grille back into place, adjusted her headwrap and stood up.

Almost immediately a dim yellow glow

filled the museum cellar. Frankie had switched on a light.

'You've obviously been here before,' said Mizz Z, surveying a wall which had a tiny red dragon spray-painted in one corner. He had flames shooting out of his mouth in the shape of a spiky letter 'F'. It was Frankie's tag. You could find it on boarded-up empty buildings; in deserted, rubble-strewn wastelands. Frankie carried a paint can with her at all times. She had one now, in a secret pocket she'd sewn into the skirt of her black frock.

Mizz Z pursed her lips. Frankie steeled herself for a stern comment – she knew that, like Mum, Mizz Z didn't approve of graffiti.

And here it came.

'Why do you mark your territory like a wild dog peeing?' demanded Mizz Z. 'That is for animals. Not people.'

'What?' said Frankie, bewildered.

But Mizz Z didn't repeat her enigmatic remarks. Instead, she turned her attention to the big wooden crates piled up in the cellar.

'*Ahhh*,' she said, her amber eye flashing in the gloom. 'Perhaps one of these crates contains the artefacts I am seeking.'

'What are these two ancient artefacts exactly?' asked Frankie. 'What part of the world do they come from?'

'They are African,' said Mizz Z. 'And actually these are not so ancient. Perhaps only a few hundred years old. Strangely, like Zilombo, they come from quite near the village where I grew up.'

Then suddenly she pounced, like a panther. Her triumphant voice came from behind a pile of crates.

'I have found them!' she said.

Chapter Five

'This is lucky,' said Mizz Z. 'They haven't put the artefacts away in a crate yet. That makes my job very simple. I shall just check them over here, then we'll go. And I can phone RAAAA about finding the Iron Dragon.'

Frankie had joined Mizz Z behind the crates. At first, she couldn't see anything in the shadows. Just a few glints of metal.

'Where are they?' she asked.

Then Mizz Z flicked another light switch she'd found and light flooded into the dark corner.

Frankie sprang backwards, startled.

A carving as tall as her brother Jin was staring at her. It had a square body and blocky hands and feet, as if it had been roughly

hacked, in a hurry, from a lump of wood. It
had jointed legs and arms, like a clumsy, life-
size puppet, and it bristled all over with bits of
sharp metal that had been hammered into its
wooden body. Its head was free of metal,
except for a crest of giant spikes that ran, like
a Mohawk, over its smooth wooden skull,
from its forehead to its spine. Its lips were
pulled back, showing two rows of yellowed
teeth, carved from bone that had once been
pure white. Each tooth was filed to a point. Its
eyes, made of bone too, were blank yellow
discs.

Now she'd got over her alarm, Frankie
went closer. 'That's a weird-looking thing,'
she said, peering at it. 'Looks like it's made
of old rubbish.'

There were even wispy old rags of material
tied around some of the metal. And what
seemed like a net, twisted around its waist like
a belt.

'It's called Avenger,' said Mizz Z coolly. 'It
once belonged to the Crocodile King.'

'What are those metal bits sticking out all over it? And who's this Crocodile King?' asked Frankie.

Mizz Z tutted at the impatience of children. 'So many questions,' she said. 'The metal bits are all sorts of things: broken tools, nails, bits of bronze necklace . . .'

'So who's this Croc King guy?' asked Frankie.

'I am about to tell you! He was a ruler, hundreds of years ago. He ruled in the mountains near my village. And he was called the Crocodile King because of his favourite mask.' From the top of a crate, Mizz Z picked up the second artefact she'd come to inspect. 'Here it is,' she said.

It was a wooden crocodile mask with a long snout and gaping jaws, lined with ferocious, jagged fangs.

'Those are real crocodile teeth,' she told Frankie. 'And when you put the mask on, you can be completely concealed.'

Frankie could see why. The mask was huge:

it covered your whole head. And attached to it were fringes of long, dangly palm-leaf fronds meant to hide your entire body, right down to your feet.

But, like Avenger, the mask was showing its age. The once bright paint had rubbed off, showing bare wood. The palm fronds were withered and brown. As Mizz Z held the mask up for Frankie to see, a tooth fell out of the jaw and rolled off into darkness.

'Not surprised they shoved the mask and Avenger down here,' said Frankie. 'They ought to chuck them out. They're falling to bits.'

'They are still precious artefacts,' Mizz Z reproved her. 'And they were dangerous once. Just like Zilombo, they could be dangerous again, if the right conditions occur. Although I must admit,' she added, 'that the chance of those conditions occurring is about ten zillion to one. So you need not worry.'

'I wasn't worrying,' said Frankie. But she was curious now. 'So why were they dangerous once?'

'In those far-off days,' Mizz Z told Frankie, 'the Crocodile King was feared by all his subjects. They quaked when they heard his name. But they quaked even more when they heard the name "Avenger".'

'But it's just a tatty old wooden statue,' said Frankie.

'Do not be deceived,' warned Mizz Z. 'Avenger was the Crocodile King's most deadly weapon. The king was afraid of his power being taken away and he saw rivals everywhere. So he sent Avenger to find them. This was his killing machine.'

'You're joking me!' said Frankie.

'I do not joke,' said Mizz Z, 'about things like that.' She continued, 'It was a strange ceremony. Every time the king wanted to kill someone he put on this mask. Then he hammered a new bit of sharp metal into his statue. As you can see.' Mizz Z indicated the metal bristling from Avenger's wooden body. 'And this had the effect of switching Avenger on, or, as one might say nowadays, activating it.'

Frankie had an avalanche of questions: 'You mean it moved? Like a robot? It went after people?'

'So the old stories say,' said Mizz Z.

'If it's a machine, what made it go? Like, clockwork or something inside it? Or magic?'

'The old stories don't explain,' said Mizz Z. 'They never do. In the old stories, things are as they are. They only say that, once the Crocodile King had switched on Avenger, the king cursed his rival. He ordered that this or that man must die, then sent Avenger to do the dirty work. And Avenger carried out his instructions.'

'*Oooo*, scary!' said Frankie sarcastically, at the same time feeling a chill chase along her spine.

'Yes, it was very scary,' agreed Mizz Z, her own voice deadly serious.

'So how did this Avenger kill them?' asked Frankie. As far as she could tell, the statue didn't have a single weapon.

'The old stories don't explain that, either,'

admitted Mizz Z. 'They just say Avenger's victims were found mysteriously dead, with not a single mark upon their bodies. Some people say they died of terror.'

'What?' scoffed Frankie. 'They can't have been *scared* of that heap of junk.'

'But all the stories agree on one thing,' continued Mizz Z, her face grim. 'They say: "*Once cursed, you are already dead.*" Because no one the Croc King cursed ever escaped Avenger. You could run to the end of the world, you could hide in the deepest caves, or on the highest mountains, but Avenger never gave up. It *always* tracked you down. And it showed no mercy. It couldn't. Because it is just a machine, with no feelings.'

Frankie stared at Avenger's wrecked face. And suddenly the statue didn't seem like a joke any more. Instead, it looked really sinister with its Mohawk crest of rusty spikes and needle-sharp teeth bared in a snarl.

'That's the stupidest thing I ever heard,'

66

she whispered as that chill clutched her again, like an icy claw.

'Perhaps it is,' agreed Mizz Z. 'But don't you want to hear how Avenger ended up here in England?'

Frankie shrugged, as if to say, 'Who cares?' But when Mizz Z spoke, she listened, twisting a loose black frill from her frock tightly round and round her wrist.

'A few hundred years ago,' said Mizz Z, 'there was a ruthless English prince who, just like the Crocodile King, was well known for wiping out all his rivals. From a travelling merchant, this evil prince came to hear of Avenger. As soon as the Crocodile King died, he sent his knights to steal it, along with the mask. They needn't have bothered, because the prince couldn't activate Avenger no matter how hard he tried – only the Crocodile King had the power to do that. But since then, Avenger has remained here in the UK, passed around with the mask from one owner to another until they both ended up in this museum.'

Frankie gave a laugh that was rather too loud and shrill. 'Hey,' she cried, grabbing the mask. 'This Avenger sounds cool. Think I could hammer in something sharp? Switch it on? Send it after this girl at school who annoys me? Just to scare her a little bit?' Grinning, she held up the mask with its trailing palm fronds. 'It's really heavy! How do you put this contraption on?'

'That is not a good idea,' warned Mizz Z.

But Frankie had already rammed the mask onto her head. It completely covered it, like a helmet. The palm-leaf cape reached to the floor and Frankie stuck her arms out between the fronds. Her eyes glittered from deep within the crocodile's jaws.

'Mizz Z?' A trembling voice came echoing from the depths of the massive mask. 'It's really dark in here.'

Suddenly Mizz Z, towering over Frankie, grabbed the crocodile head and yanked it off. Frankie's face appeared, blinking in the light. She looked dazed, as if she had no idea where she was, or what had happened.

'Avenger cannot be used to settle silly children's quarrels,' snapped Mizz Z, her amber eye flashing like a fierce tigress. 'Do you hear me, Frankie? I am speaking to you!'

Frankie came sharply back to her senses, startled by Mizz Z's anger. 'I was only messing about,' she protested. 'I wasn't *serious*. I mean, it wouldn't have worked. Would it? I couldn't really have switched on Avenger?'

'No, it wouldn't have worked,' said Mizz Z, in softer tones. 'As I said before, only the Crocodile King can switch on Avenger. And he's been dead for hundreds of years. But one must not mess around with ancient artefacts. At least, not the ones I inspect. All of them carry a risk.' And she laid the mask carefully back on the crate.

She didn't mention the Crocodile King's spirit which, according to the stories Granny Zauyamakanda used to tell, was still around, shut up inside an ancient baobab.

Even if it is true, Mizz Z told herself, *his*

spirit is thousands of miles away in Africa, in my old village. It can't harm anyone here. 'Let's go back to the Money Tree bakery,' she said, her voice as cool as a chilled watermelon. 'I have seen all I want to see. These artefacts are perfectly safe.'

Then Frankie said, 'What's that noise?'

It came again – a squeaking sound.

'*Hmmm*,' said Mizz Z. 'I believe someone is coming in this direction.'

The squeaking got louder, then stopped, right outside the cellar door. Frankie heard the door creaking. There was no time to crawl back to the Money Tree cellar.

'Hide!' hissed Mizz Z. 'Someone is coming in.'

They ducked down behind two big crates and Frankie peeped out between them. In the dim glow she saw an old guy come into the cellar, pushing a flat trolley with squeaky wheels.

He seemed to know exactly what he was looking for. He wheeled the trolley straight over to Avenger and the Crocodile King's mask.

Frankie held her breath. He was very close now – she could smell the fustiness, like mouldy old books, that wafted from his suit. She could even read the identity card pinned to his lapel that said: DR ANTHONY CRAMP. CURATOR OF ANCIENT ARTEFACTS.

But Dr Cramp, the curator, didn't look around. He wasn't expecting anyone else to be in the cellar. No one ever came down here except him. And, besides, he was on a very important mission. He'd been preparing for this day for some time. Planning it had taken every penny of his life savings.

Frankie heard him muttering something. She thought, *Who's he talking to?* Until she realized he was speaking to Avenger.

'We'll show him,' the curator told the battered wooden statue. 'We'll teach that jumped-up new director a lesson. He says you're not *exciting* enough. That you're just a boring lump of wood. Well, after tonight he's

71

going to get a very nasty surprise.' Dr Cramp pulled on two thick gardening gloves. Wheezing with the effort, he lifted Avenger's spiky body and, staggering a little, loaded it onto the trolley. Then he laid the Crocodile King's mask beside it. 'Show time!' he said.

The door closed and Frankie heard the trolley squeaking away from the cellar.

Mizz Z rose up from behind the crates. Frankie came out too. 'What a loony old guy,' she grinned.

But Mizz Z wasn't smiling. Her face was thoughtful. 'I think this man is up to no good,' she told Frankie. She carefully opened the cellar door and peered out into the shadowy passage beyond. From somewhere, Frankie heard the grind and whirr of machinery. Mizz Z opened the door wide. 'It's OK,' she said to Frankie. 'He's taken the trolley up in the service lift.'

Frankie came out of the cellar and walked to the lift with Mizz Z. They saw 'G' light up.

'He's getting out on the ground floor of the

museum,' said Mizz Z. She seemed undecided. 'It's all probably perfectly innocent. Although perhaps we'd better see what he's up to. Wait a minute – didn't you say earlier that Jin and your dad are in the museum? What are they doing here?'

'My dad's a rodent control technician . . .' began Frankie. She paused, half expecting Mizz Z to laugh and exclaim, 'A *what*?'

But Mizz Z didn't react. She seemed to be only half listening, busy with her own thoughts.

'Anyway,' Frankie rushed on, 'Dad got a call when we were in the burger bar. There's a rat in a toilet. A toilet in a *tree* that's come all the way from Africa.'

At last Mizz Z gave Frankie her full attention, turning that piercing eye upon her like a laser beam. 'Do you know anything more about this tree?' she demanded.

'I wasn't really listening,' shrugged Frankie.

'Try to remember,' insisted Mizz Z. 'This may be very important.'

Frankie searched her brain. 'It's their newest exhibit,' she finally came up with. 'And Dad said something about the toilet being nailed up, inside the tree? It all sounds crazy, if you ask me.'

But it made perfect sense to Mizz Z. Instantly her mind flashed back to when she'd been eleven years old, standing with her dad and Kapito at the opening ceremony of the public convenience. And how Mr Ulili had had a dreadful scare inside the baobab and scarpered in his limo at top speed.

'I told them,' Gran had said afterwards, 'not to mess around with that baobab. Mark my words, that Crocodile King is still hungry for power, even though he's dead. But no one listens to us old people any more.'

Mizz Z hadn't known what to believe. But some nights later she'd crept out at the dead of night and helped Gran nail up Mr Ulili's public convenience.

This surely couldn't be the same tree. The tree the king's body had been buried inside?

The tree Gran had said his spirit still haunted?

It can't be, Mizz Z decided. *For the tree to arrive in this city. In the very same museum where the Crocodile King's mask and Avenger are stored. That would be an unbelievable coincidence.*

But, all the same, however unlikely, a Chief Inspector always takes precautions. If the king, even in spirit form, was ever reunited with his old possessions, Mizz Z knew chaos and death would follow.

'Wait here,' she told Frankie. 'I'll take the stairs. I think I'll keep an eye on this curator.'

Chapter Six

Jin and Dad were still hunting for the Giant Pouched Rat. At first Jin went crashing frantically around the exhibition hall, peering into the pharaoh's golden toilet, lifting up the seat of the Japanese karaoke loo to see if the poor, frightened creature had hidden inside.

He didn't find the rat. All he succeeded in doing was knocking over a display of 'Toilet Rolls from Around the World' and sending them flying.

Frustrated, he smacked his hand off his forehead. 'You're so clumsy! You'll never find him!' he scolded himself.

Dad loomed up beside him. 'Doesn't matter if you're clumsy,' he told Jin. 'That's got nothing to do with rat-catching. To catch a rat you have to track him down, use your senses.'

'What senses?' said Jin.

'Well, your eyes for a start. When I'm tracking rats I look for gnaw marks. Rats can't help chewing on stuff – wires, wood, concrete – as they pass. Then I look for droppings, or the greasy marks from their fur. Then I listen. You might hear him scuffling or scratching or squeaking. Then smell. Rats have this musty smell. Once you've smelled it, you never forget it. You got all that?'

Jin nodded. 'I think so.' He'd never thought rat-catching could be this complicated.

'Right,' said Dad. 'Let's go find some rat signs!'

Jin took a few deep breaths to calm himself, then started to look for gnaw marks. As he searched, Jin marvelled again at how confident and sure of himself Dad was. Not as superconfident as Mizz Z, though, he decided.

Then suddenly, as if he'd magicked her up by the power of thought, Mizz Z came through a swing door, right in front of him. Jin's jaw dropped. For a few seconds, he hardly knew if she was real.

But then she said, in those familiar ice-cool tones, 'Why are you staring? You look as if you've seen a ghost.'

'Mizz Z! I was just thinking about you!' stammered Jin.

Frankie appeared through the same door. 'Hi, bro',' she said. 'We've just come up the stairs from the cellar.'

'Frankie, I told you to wait downstairs,' said Mizz Z.

'Sorry,' said Frankie. 'I didn't hear.'

Jin, still gaping at Mizz Z, said, 'What were you doing in the cellar?'

'I am on a mission,' explained Mizz Z. 'For RAAAA.' Then her rather stern face broke into a warm-hearted smile. 'My little friend Jin,' she said. 'It's so good to see you again. But what have you done to your nose?'

'Eh?' said Jin. He put his hand up and felt the skull plaster. He'd forgotten about that. 'Oh, nothing,' he shrugged. 'I had a fight with a cupboard door. How are the Lakeside Queens doing?'

'They won the Schoolgirls' Football League last month!' Mizz Z told them, her face lighting up with sudden joy. 'Listen!' She took her phone out of her pocket and played them a few seconds of wild whooping and clapping. 'That is the sound of their fans celebrating. It is my new ring tone.'

'They're going crazy!' said Jin.

'They are football fanatics, like me,' said Mizz Z approvingly. Then she switched off the cheers and added, 'And guess what. Betsy Zauyamakanda, my niece and our star striker, has a trial for the ladies' national team!'

Frankie whistled in admiration.

'Wow, awesome!' said Jin.

'I know.' Mizz Z nodded, obviously thrilled to bits.

Dad came striding up. Instantly Mizz Z

swapped from proud football coach to dignified Chief Inspector.

'Are you going to introduce me?' Dad asked Jin.

'Oh, sorry, Dad. This is Mizz Z. Mizz Z, this is Dad.'

Dad had never met Mizz Z before. But he knew all about the intrepid Chief Inspector who, on her last visit to the city, had saved his baby son's life. He pumped her hand up and down in his huge paw: 'Mizz Z, it's a great honour!'

Mizz Z nodded graciously, as if she agreed. Then she put her phone away and scanned the exhibition hall. 'We are looking for a man wheeling a trolley,' she told Jin and Dad.

'I just saw the curator with a trolley,' said Jin. 'He came out of the lift. But he went off somewhere.' Jin had only got a glimpse. He'd stayed out of the way. 'I didn't let him see me,' he added. 'He hates kids, that guy.'

Then Mizz Z spotted the baobab tree in the little side room. She recognized it immediately. There could be no mistake.

'It's the tree the Crocodile King was buried in,' she whispered. Someone had ripped off the planks that she and her grandmother had nailed across the door all those years ago.

Inside Mizz Z's head, alarm bells were ringing, yet her composed features hardly changed. What if Gran had been right about the king's spirit still being inside? Only Jin, an expert at reading faces, saw a tiny nerve flutter in Mizz Z's cheek under her black eye patch, and knew she was getting worried about something.

He was about to say, 'What's up, Mizz Z?' when they heard a squeaking sound.

'Dad! It's the Giant Pouched Rat!' said Jin, overjoyed. 'We've found him.'

Frankie said, 'Giant Pouched *what*?'

While Mizz Z said, 'That is no rat. Except of the human kind. We must conceal ourselves immediately!' She slid back behind the swing door. Jin and Frankie joined her without question. They knew from past experience that Mizz Z didn't give urgent orders for nothing.

Dad's eyebrows shot up in surprise. He said, half laughing, 'Why are we hiding?' But then he did the same. There was something about Mizz Z's voice that told him she wasn't joking.

Through a glass panel in the swing door they could see what was going on in the main hall. They also had a clear view of the baobab tree, in its little side room.

Suddenly Dr Cramp appeared from a corridor, wheeling his trolley across the hall. He seemed to be making for that little side room. Through the glass panel, Mizz Z checked what was on the trolley. Avenger was there, his spiky body standing upright, with the crocodile mask laid beside him. But the doctor had been to fetch something else. Beside the mask was a hammer and a little glass jar of nails.

'Oh, no,' breathed Mizz Z. That nerve in her cheek was twitching like mad. 'What does this silly man think he is doing?'

And even from behind the swing door, Jin sensed the tension building. Those sinister vibes he'd felt when they'd first entered the museum were crackling in the air like electricity. With each step the curator took towards the baobab they seemed to grow stronger and more menacing. Jin could feel his hair lifting from his scalp, as if something awful was about to happen. Although he had no idea what it was.

'What's going on?' whispered Frankie.

Grim-faced, Mizz Z answered, 'That man is messing with powers he does not understand.'

Dr Cramp lifted the mask with its dangling palm fronds. In one swift movement, he crammed it over his head. Now he had mean little crocodile eyes and a vicious snaggle-toothed snout. The palm fronds covered the rest of his body like a long cloak.

Mizz Z sprang into action. She burst through the swing door and sprinted across the hall. 'Stay there!' she yelled over her shoulder to Jin, Dad and Frankie, who were gaping after her.

Dr Cramp, hidden from head to foot,

whirled round, his palm-frond cloak flying. His hand reached out to open the door in the baobab's trunk.

'No!' yelled Mizz Z as she was running. She skidded to a stop beside the curator. 'Have you any idea,' she gasped, 'what you are doing?'

A voice, dry as dust, came from inside the crocodile mask. 'Of course I have,' it told Mizz Z. 'I am the world's leading expert on African artefacts. And who are you?'

Mizz Z's chin tilted proudly upwards. 'I am the Chief Inspector of RAAAA,' she informed him.

Fear flickered like a snake's tongue in Dr Cramp's brain. Wasn't RAAAA the organization that boy had mentioned earlier? But what did they matter? Nothing could stop him now. He was so near his goal. His hand sneaked again towards the door in the trunk.

'Stop!' commanded Mizz Z. She still couldn't believe that he really understood the consequences of his actions.

Meanwhile, behind the swing door, Dad admitted, 'I'm totally confused.'

'That's OK,' said Jin. 'I feel like that most of the time.'

Dad appealed to Frankie. 'Can you tell me what this is all about?'

Frankie frowned. She wasn't laughing about Avenger now, or calling it a heap of junk. 'It's about that statue,' she told him. 'The one on the trolley. Mizz Z came specially to inspect it. She's worried that it could be dangerous.'

Dad was still puzzled. He said, 'Dangerous? Is it a Health and Safety risk? Is it because it's spiky and kids could cut themselves?'

Jin glanced at Frankie's serious face. 'No,' he guessed. 'It's much more dangerous than that. Like, life-and-death dangerous. Else Mizz Z wouldn't be involved.'

Frankie nodded gravely in agreement. 'Jin's right,' she said. And in a few brief words she told them all she knew about the Crocodile King's mask and Avenger. 'So Avenger's got ancient powers,' she concluded, feeling that icy chill down her backbone again. 'Once it's activated, it tracks people down. They never, ever escape.'

Dad stared at her, amazed. 'I don't believe it. Who told you all that rubbish?'

'Mizz Z did,' said Frankie.

Jin said, 'Dad, you'd better believe it.' He pushed at the swing door. 'Let's go.'

'She said to stay here,' Frankie pointed out.

'So?' said Jin. 'She might need some help.'

The three of them crept across the main hall towards the small room. Jin felt his nerves stretched to snapping point. As if a bomb was ticking, counting down the last seconds before it exploded.

'Take off that mask!' Mizz Z ordered Dr Cramp. 'I thought *you* were the expert? Surely you know what could happen? If not, I will explain it in simple terms! That tree may contain the Crocodile King's spirit. There is a way his spirit can live again, become flesh and blood. That can happen if someone wears his mask near the baobab. Just like you are doing now. The old stories tell us that the king's spirit will leave the tree and enter the mind and body of the mask-wearer. In this case, that is you! He will take over your body and use it to activate Avenger, his killing machine—'

'But that is exactly what I want to happen,' interrupted the curator, scuttling away from Mizz Z to the other side of the room. His thin, reedy voice suddenly became loud and triumphant. He pointed to the sign on the baobab. 'I am that *unknown benefactor*!' he boasted. 'It was I who arranged for the baobab to be brought here.'

Mizz Z stared at Dr Cramp in disbelief. 'You have planned all this *deliberately*? You *want* the king to take over your body? To activate Avenger?'

'Actually,' Dr Cramp's arrogant voice came from the mask, 'it won't happen quite like that. After Avenger has been activated, I shall drive the king out of my mind. Then I shall be Avenger's master. And it will do my bidding.'

'You are completely insane,' said Mizz Z. 'Do you really think you, a puny human, can control ancient powers? They are stronger than you can ever imagine!'

Suddenly the others appeared in the small room. Dr Cramp recognized Jin and Dad. 'What are you still doing here?' he demanded angrily. 'I thought you'd gone long ago.'

'We were looking for a Giant Pouched—' Jin started to say.

Then, from inside the baobab, came a sudden loud banging and crashing. All their eyes shot towards the tree. The crashing sounds came again, like a caged lion that finally scents freedom after being shut up for years and years.

'It is the Crocodile King's spirit,' whispered Mizz Z, suddenly certain that Granny Zauya-makanda had been right all along.

She was about to dive across the room at Dr Cramp and snatch the mask off his head, but then the door to the baobab burst open and a shriek of triumph made Jin nearly jump out his skin.

He stared around wildly. 'Where'd that come from?'

But there was nothing to see, just a brief rippling in the air between the baobab and the curator. Then there was silence.

'What's happened?' said Frankie.

They all stared at the masked figure. Dr Cramp didn't seem any different. They could still see his scuffed shoes and glimpse his rumpled suit between the palm fronds.

Then, 'Look at his eyes,' said Jin who, with his face-reading skills, was the first to notice the change.

Dr Cramp's pale green eyes stared back at them from deep inside the crocodile jaws. But they had a fiery glint in them that hadn't been there before. Then a voice boomed out. And it wasn't anything like the curator's fussy, flute-like tones. It was a deep, menacing growl.

'It's the Crocodile King,' Mizz Z whispered again, in the same awe-stricken voice. 'He has taken over Dr Cramps's body. The Crocodile King lives again!'

Chapter Seven

Suddenly the growl coming from Dr Cramp's mouth rose to an angry shriek. The Crocodile King, who lived inside Dr Cramp's body, was yelling at them, jabbing his fingers.

Frantically Mizz Z thought, *What language is he speaking?* Then she caught a few familiar words and realized it was a very old form of Chewa, the language of her own home village and all her family.

To Jin's amazement, the proud Mizz Z sank to her knees. She bowed her head. 'He's saying we must kneel,' she hissed at the three of them.

'No way,' said Frankie, tossing her head defiantly. But she still plonked herself down, along with Jin. Sequins pinged off her dress and glittered on the floor like tiny black stars.

'I don't kneel to anyone,' Dad insisted.

'Please do as I say, Mr Sparks,' said Mizz Z urgently. 'Kneel for the Crocodile King. If you want to stay alive.'

Dad muttered, 'I can't believe I'm doing this.' Sighing, he slumped to his knees, the steel toes of his rat-fighting boots ringing on the tiled floor.

Keeping her eyes low, Mizz Z spoke humbly in Chewa to the Crocodile King. She told him that they were his loyal subjects. That their only wish was to serve him. That there was no way they would ever challenge his power.

And, at first, her words seemed to calm him. Jin raised his eyes, dared to take a peek.

The king, inside Dr Cramp's body, was seated on the trolley like a royal throne. Avenger stood beside him, guarding him, as it always had hundreds of years ago. The crocodile mask swivelled towards the four kneeling figures. Its snout stopped at Mizz Z. That domineering voice came again, rumbling like thunder around the room. It was clear he was giving orders. And that he was used to being instantly obeyed.

'I don't like this king dude,' Frankie hissed to Mizz Z. 'What's he saying now?'

'He is demanding to know my family name,' Mizz Z whispered back.

'Who's he think he is?' fumed Frankie. 'Giving *you* orders! You're the Chief Inspector!'

'Frankie, keep calm,' said Mizz Z. 'It will be best for all of us. We mustn't anger him. If he thinks we are enemies, he will activate Avenger.'

But Frankie was already speaking up. 'Mizz Z is a Zauyamakanda,' she said defiantly. 'Not that it's any of your business.'

The name had an explosive effect. 'Zauyamakanda!' howled the king. Then he seemed to go berserk. He leaped up from the trolley, the palm-frond cape swirling. He was shrieking even louder this time, froth flying from the crocodile's jaws, jabbing an accusing finger at Mizz Z.

Mizz Z looked startled, protested, half rose to her feet.

But the king had seen the nails and hammer. He tipped out the jar, sending silver nails skittering everywhere. He grabbed one. Mizz Z ran towards him but she was too late. He was already hammering it manically into Avenger's wooden chest, among the other bits of spiky metal.

Mizz Z fell back and stared, aghast, as the Crocodile King stopped shrieking and started to drone some words in a low, chanting voice. Jin heard 'Zauyamakanda' repeated several times.

'What's he saying? Tell us!' begged Frankie.

'He has just cursed me! Me and all my family,' Mizz Z replied, stunned. 'Why has he done that? We Zauyamakandas have never done him any harm.'

Jin stared at Mizz Z, hardly understanding. But Frankie remembered Mizz Z's grim words: *Once cursed, you are already dead.*

Her humble act over, Mizz Z went on the

attack. She sprang again at the Crocodile King. This mission had suddenly become personal.

'Take that curse back!' she demanded.

Mizz Z was tall, even taller in her platform-soled flip-flops. She grasped the mask and the king screamed, outraged that anyone should touch his royal person. He wasn't expecting it or he would have fought like a tiger to prevent her.

'Be gone!' Mizz Z commanded the Crocodile King's spirit as she ripped off the mask in one swift movement.

From the shoes up Dr Cramp was revealed again – first his baggy grey suit, then his whiskery face. He blinked and looked dazed. 'What happened?' he quavered in his thin, reedy voice. Then he collapsed onto the trolley. His eyes were tight shut. His limbs quivered once, twice, then stayed still.

Mizz Z wasn't concerned with Dr Cramp. She was staring – her throat dry, her heart hammering – at Avenger. But the spiky statue didn't move – not one centimetre.

One minute passed, then two. She checked Avenger's feet, its wooden fingers. Not a twitch.

Jin was whispering, horrified, 'Is the curator dead?'

Quickly Mizz Z lifted Dr Cramp's eyelids, felt his pulse. Then her gaze switched back to Avenger.

'Well, is he dead?' Jin demanded.

'No,' said Mizz Z, all the while staring at the spiky statue. 'He's just fainted from the shock of the Crocodile King invading his body. But the king has left now. He can only stay in someone's body as long as they are wearing the mask. Unfortunately it was long enough for him to activate Avenger—'

'Avenger doesn't look activated to me,' Frankie interrupted.

'It doesn't to me, either,' said Jin.

He detected two expressions pass over Mizz Z's hawk-like features. The first was puzzlement. The second was hope.

More minutes passed. Still Avenger didn't move.

'Can I get up now?' Dad was saying. 'My knees can't stand much more of this.' But no one took any notice.

Jin's sharp eyes spotted that, as the minutes dragged by, the fluttering nerve beneath Mizz Z's eye patch was pulsing more slowly. Jin felt his own racing heart slowing down too, as if to beat to the same rhythm.

More time passed. Still no movement.

Finally Mizz Z spoke. 'I don't think Avenger's switched on,' she told them, relief washing over her face like sunshine.

You never know, she was thinking, *with these ancient artefacts. Some keep their power for hundreds, even thousands, of years. Some don't. Maybe they'd never had it in the first place. Many of those old stories got it wrong.*

'No, it's *definitely* not activated,' decided Mizz Z. 'So it can't carry out the king's curse, can it? We Zauyamakandas are safe.'

Frantically Jin sucked in some air. He hadn't realized it, but he'd been holding his breath until he'd gone almost blue. Then he had a coughing fit.

Frankie slapped him hard on the back. 'You all right, bro'?'

'Yeah, you don't need to break my ribs!'

'So, if he's not inside Doctor Cramp, where's this Crocodile King supposed to have gone now?' asked Dad.

Mizz Z ignored the disbelief in Dad's voice. 'The king's spirit is inside his tree,' she answered, nodding her head towards the door in the baobab. It had closed again, but she didn't bother to open it – she knew there'd be nothing to see except the toilet and basin. 'His spirit must have a home. It must be inside whoever wears the mask. Or inside the baobab. Although I believe another tree would do just as well. So long as it is ancient.'

Mizz Z was using her brisk, efficient Chief Inspector's voice again, as if to assure them. 'The panic's over. We can all calm down.' She laid the empty crocodile mask carefully on the floor, smoothing out the palm fronds, checking for damage. '*Tut tut*,' she said. 'Some have broken off. It will have to be repaired.'

But Frankie leaped up off her knees. 'Repaired?!' she cried passionately. 'No way! That mask should be destroyed! Then no one can ever wear it. And that Croc King can never take over anyone's body or activate Avenger. Or curse people ever again.'

'Frankie's right,' Jin agreed. 'Destroy it. Smash it to bits. And Avenger too.'

'No,' replied Mizz Z firmly. 'I hear what you are both saying. But all ancient artefacts are precious, no matter how dangerous. They are our heritage and it's a Chief Inspector's job to protect them. Besides,' she added, 'these two are perfectly safe. It seems the king can't use them to regain his power.'

'You mean, he *definitely* can't activate that wooden freak?' asked Jin anxiously.

'I have just said so,' Mizz Z told him. 'But see for yourself.'

Jin stared again at Avenger. Its face was

fixed in the same snarling expression. Its fingers were still and clenched at its sides.

Nothing's happening, Jin reassured himself. *It's just a lump of wood*. His tension was rushing away now, like water down a drain. He was almost relaxed again. Or as relaxed as you ever got when Mizz Z was around. Then, with his keen eye for detail, he saw something he hadn't noticed.

Avenger's got some jewellery, he thought, surprised.

Not an earring exactly, but an ear plug – a slim tube of yellow bone slotted through a hole in its right ear lobe. The ornament seemed too fine and delicate for such a roughly hacked figure, so skilfully carved it was almost transparent.

Jin noticed it, then forgot it. It didn't seem that important. Not now the danger was past.

Frankie was busy whacking floor dust off her jet-black skirts. 'What was the Croc King's curse, exactly?' she asked Mizz Z.

'For heaven's sake,' said Dad, hauling

himself off his knees. 'There wasn't any curse. Or any Crocodile King. Just some crazy old curator dressed in a crocodile mask, who pretended to be him.'

Mizz Z shot Dad a pitying look that said: *How little you understand.* Then she answered Frankie. 'The king cursed me and all Zauya-makandas in my family. He said every one of us will be eliminated. With me first on the list. He said Avenger will not stop until none of us remain on Earth.'

'But that's a terrible curse!' said Jin.

Mizz Z nodded grimly. 'My entire family could have been wiped out. If Avenger had been activated.'

Dad was checking his rat-catching belt. 'Right,' he told Jin. 'Let's find that Giant Pouched Rat and get out of here.'

But suddenly Jin gasped, 'Its eyes! Look at Avenger's eyes!'

Everyone stared at Avenger, except the doctor, who was still unconscious.

'They're lit up,' whispered Frankie.

'How'd it *do* that?' said Dad, some of the disbelief fading from his voice.

Avenger's face was still fixed in the same snarl. Its body didn't move, not a millimetre, but its bone eye discs shone out with an eerie glow. As if someone had switched on a light inside its wooden skull.

'It *is* activated!' said Mizz Z, unable to hide the dread in her voice. It had just taken a long time warming up, like an old car that hasn't been driven for ages.

With a rasp of rusty metal, Avenger's Mohawk crest swivelled round. The statue fixed Mizz Z with a yellow glare, like a guided mission locking onto its target. Its eyes were luminous now, sending out twin rays as dazzling as laser beams.

Mizz Z was already backing away, out of the small room. She stumbled into the door frame. It knocked her headwrap lopsided, and then the wrap slid off entirely, showing her braided hair. But Mizz Z didn't stop to pick it up.

Jin had forgotten he was still on his knees. He lurched to his feet. 'Where are you going?' he asked Mizz Z frantically.

Her eyes fixed on Avenger, Mizz Z declared, 'I am going to find somewhere to hide.'

Frankie was recalling, with horror, what else Mizz Z had said. *You could run to the end of the world, but Avenger always tracked you down.* 'I'll come with you. I know all the best places to hide in this city,' she blurted out.

'That is not allowed,' said Mizz Z. 'I am the Chief Inspector. I alone must run the risks.'

Then Jin heard the sound of grating metal. His eyes swung again to Avenger. It was moving! First its knees bent. Then it climbed slowly off the trolley, its movements jerky, like a mad robot. It crouched, gazing around. Mizz Z was already running through the main hall, her flip-flops slapping on the tiles.

Ignoring Jin's shouts of, 'Wait for me!' Frankie took off after Mizz Z, dashed out of the small room and disappeared. They heard doors bang and the sound of their footsteps faded into the distance.

Mr Sparks stood gazing open-mouthed after his daughter. His brain was totally scrambled. Nothing seemed to make any sense. Long-dead kings putting curses on living people? Lumps of wood coming alive? 'I don't believe any of this,' he whispered, shaking his head. 'It's not happening.'

'It is, Dad, it is!' someone was screaming at him. Dad looked down. Jin was desperately shaking his arm.

Jin had no problem believing, not after his last amazing adventure with Mizz Z. Besides, when he was tiny, it had often seemed to Jin that things came alive. The pavement leaped to trip him up, doors whacked him on the nose, and pencils went all wriggly, like worms, in his hand.

'Come on, Dad,' he pleaded. 'This is serious. We've got to do something. That thing's going after Mizz Z.'

Avenger's joints hadn't moved for

hundreds of years. They were stiff and creaky. Now it was lurching across the floor of the small room. It didn't once glance at Dad and Jin. They weren't its concern, so long as they didn't get in its way.

It didn't immediately follow Mizz Z. As Jin watched, hot and cold shocks chasing over his body, Avenger stopped in the doorway. It picked up Mizz Z's headwrap in its clumsy fingers and put it up near its nose, sniffing in the fragrance of frangipani flowers from Mizz Z's perfumed hair oil.

Using its sharp filed teeth Avenger then ripped a piece from the headwrap and hung the pink, orange and yellow scrap of material on the new silver nail in its chest. It bent its great spiky head to sniff its new rag, as if to remind itself of the flowery smell, then picked up the scent in the air.

And it set off to hunt Mizz Z down.

Once out of the small room, it swerved sharp left and Jin lost sight of it.

'Come on, Dad,' he said, tugging on his

father's arm again. 'We've got to follow it.'
But Dad still seemed dazed, lost in a dream.

Avenger creaked away through the main
hall, its gleaming eyes staring straight ahead.
There was a toilet blocking its path. Made of
china, painted with beautiful blue flowers,
it had once belonged to a Russian tsarina.
Using its wooden arm like a club, Avenger
dashed it out of its way and the toilet flew into
the wall and shattered into a thousand pieces.
In the middle of the debris sat the Giant
Pouched Rat, who had been trembling inside
the bowl. Dazed, it shook china fragments out
of its fur and crept away to find another hiding
place.

Avenger marched jerkily on, its brick-
shaped wooden feet clacking on the tiles.
Nothing, no one, would stop it in its pursuit
of Mizz Z. It would never give up until it had
found her. And, after that, it would deal –
one by one – with the rest of her family.

'Dad,' said Jin, 'I'm leaving you here. I'm
going after Mizz Z on my own. Right?'

At last, Dad seemed to snap out of his trance. 'Was that statue *alive*?' he asked Jin.

Jin was ace at reading faces, but he hadn't seen anything human in Avenger's features. There'd been no pity or pain; no happiness or fear.

'No,' Jin said. 'It's just a machine like Mizz Z said, a machine that hunts people down for the Crocodile King. He switches it on, gives it instructions and off it goes.'

'How come you understand all this?' asked Dad.

'I don't *understand* it,' said Jin. 'I just know that's how it is, that's all.'

'But it's so *weird*,' said Dad. 'It feels like the whole world's gone mad.'

'You'd better get used to it, Dad,' advised Jin. ''Cos it happens a lot with Mizz Z.'

A groan came from the trolley. Both of them had forgotten about Dr Cramp. Dad went rushing over.

'Don't waste time on him,' urged Jin, jigging about with frustration. 'He caused all this trouble. Let's get going – we'll lose them.'

But Dad shook the curator by the shoulder. He said, 'Are you OK?'

'This is all your fault!' Jin told Dr Cramp.

The Crocodile King had only briefly taken over his mind, but it seemed to have left Dr Cramp a broken man. His pale green eyes were flickering around. All his triumph had gone. Instead, he moaned weakly, 'What have I done?'

'Just what you wanted,' shouted Jin. 'The Crocodile King activated Avenger. But then he cursed Mizz Z and all her family and sent Avenger after her. Are you happy now?'

Dr Cramp feebly raised his head. 'I didn't mean for this to happen. I thought I could take control of Avenger,' he moaned. 'Send it to get rid of the new director.'

'You wanted it to *kill* the director?' said Jin, appalled.

'No, no,' insisted Dr Cramp. 'I just wanted it to *scare* him, that's all. Chase him away, so he'd leave me and my artefacts in peace. But the ancient powers were far too strong. I didn't realize . . .' His voice faded away. He slumped back again on the trolley.

Jin shook his limp body. 'You didn't even say sorry!'

'Leave him alone,' said Dad, pulling Jin away. 'He can't do any harm now. He's just a sad old man.' To Dr Cramp he said, 'Can you hear me? We'll come back for you later.' Back in action-man mode, Dad now strode out into the main hall.

Jin was about to follow when a sudden thought struck him. Should he take the crocodile mask with him? What if Dr Cramp did put it on again? And the Croc King took over his body? The last time that happened the king had activated Avenger and sent it after Mizz Z. What other awful things would he do if he got a second chance to become flesh and blood?

'You coming, Jin?' yelled Dad.

Jin had to make a quick decision. The curator lay on the trolley, his eyes closed. He didn't look like he could jiggle his little finger, let alone lift that heavy mask over his head.

And he's probably learned his lesson, thought Jin, *not to mess any more with the Crocodile King*.

Also, Jin didn't want to lug the mask around with him. It was old and fragile. Mizz Z would be most displeased if it got damaged. And Jin was a particularly accident-prone kid. Things just seemed to come apart in his hands.

Leave it, Jin decided. He was desperate to get out of that little room, away from those creepy vibes that made your skin crawl. He hurried through the main hall. There was no sign of Mizz Z, or Frankie, or Avenger, but Dad was waiting by the swing door down to the museum cellar.

Behind Jin, all was silence inside the little room. Then suddenly a sound came from inside the baobab.

It was a low, blood-curdling chuckle.

Chapter Eight

Frankie and Mizz Z had a few minutes' lead on Avenger.

'This way,' said Frankie, about to duck through the swing door that led back down to the cellars. 'We can escape through the bakery into Chinatown.'

Mizz Z clutched Frankie's arm. 'No!' was her urgent reply. 'Avenger is after me, but heaven help anyone who gets in its way. We must lead it right away from people, to empty places.'

Frankie stared around, her brain racing, trying to think of somewhere like that. She knew plenty of forgotten, deserted places around the city. But were there any nearby?

Then suddenly she had a brainwave. 'Come

on,' she said, dashing towards the swing door.

'I told you, we can't go back the way we came,' protested Mizz Z.

'We're not,' said Frankie.

She raced past the swing door. In a small alcove, further on, there was a staircase going up. Frankie started climbing.

Before she followed, Mizz Z took one swift glance back across the main hall. Avenger was blocking the doorway of the small room, its spiky back towards her. It picked something off the floor with its chunky wooden fingers. Mizz Z's heart clenched when she saw what it was.

You shouldn't have left your headwrap behind, she scolded herself.

But it was too late now. Avenger would use her clothing as a tracking aid. Those wispy old rags all over its body, tied around bits of rusty metal, showed it had done this many times in the past. Each one of those rags represented a person – someone the Croc King had cursed and sent Avenger to hunt down. The old stories said not a single one had lived to tell the tale.

Like Frankie, Mizz Z couldn't help wondering what on earth had happened to them. 'Get a grip, A. J. Zauyamakanda,' she warned herself sternly. She must put all personal fears aside. She must keep a cool head and think like a Chief Inspector. But Avenger was turning jerkily round. Any second now it would see her.

Mizz Z dashed up the stairs. She saw Frankie's crow-black dress with its tentacle frills whisk round a corner. The staircases got narrower and narrower. Finally Mizz Z caught up with Frankie on a landing: 'Where are we going?' she demanded.

'To the roof,' said Frankie. 'You wanted an empty place.'

'But if Avenger follows us, we'll be trapped.'

'No, we won't,' said Frankie. 'There's a way down. Trust me.'

Amazingly, considering Mizz Z's proud

independence and Frankie's prickly, suspicious nature, a special trust and respect had grown between them during their last adventure. So Mizz Z didn't question Frankie any further. She just said, 'Lead the way, then.' It seemed Frankie had been here before; Mizz Z had stopped being surprised at the weird places in this city Frankie knew about.

Frankie ran ahead along a corridor, her biker boots thudding on bare floorboards.

'*Shhh*,' called Mizz Z softly. 'It will hear you.'

Frankie turned, her heart thumping. She felt suddenly sick and shaky. 'It's coming after us?'

'Of course,' said Mizz Z, keeping her voice rock-steady. 'It's coming, all right. Avenger is relentless. But it is creaky and slow after hundreds of years without moving. That gives us an advantage.'

They hurried on along a passage with shelves of dusty, forgotten exhibits, like boxes of animal bones and pots and containers whose labels had long ago faded so that no one now knew what was inside. Then they started climbing up the stairs again.

A floor below them, Avenger was tracking them down. It had lost, for a moment, the frangipani scent. So it had followed the clumping, above it, of Frankie's boots. Now that had gone. For seconds, Avenger hesitated on the landing. Which way had they headed?

With a grating sound of rusty metal, its head swivelled upwards and its blank eyes gleamed like golden fire.

Strangely Avenger had something in common with Jin. As well as following signs, it could – when it got close enough to its quarry – pick up moods, especially fear. It had had plenty of practice detecting fear, because back in the old days, when the Croc King ruled, that had been the main emotion felt by people when Avenger was hot on their trail.

Mizz Z had armed herself against fear. She'd learned to block it out of her mind. But

Frankie didn't have such iron self-control and Avenger was close enough now to feel her terror. Avenger had formidable ancient powers – it was the best tracker anywhere in the world, ever. When it got closer, it would even be able to detect Frankie's fast-beating heart and the blood pulsing through her veins.

But Mizz Z was right; Avenger's stiff joints were slowing it down. They were in danger of locking up altogether.

Avenger lurched past the shelves crammed with dusty exhibits and suddenly stopped dead. It had smelled something familiar – animal fat. It didn't mess about searching in containers. It simply swept them all off the shelves. An Egyptian jar smashed at its feet, spilling out a shrivelled mummy heart. Avenger crushed it under its foot. It crouched instead to pick up a tube made of tree bark and ripped it apart. This was what it was looking for – bear grease that Native American braves had once used to shine their hair when they were going to war.

Avenger got handfuls of the slippery grease and smeared it all over its body, working it deep into all its stiff joints until they moved smoothly like a well-oiled machine.

There was a little bit of bear grease left and Avenger used this to shine its Mohawk, making the old, rusty metal gleam. Then it was on the trail again. Following Frankie's fear, it sprinted along the corridor on its freshly greased legs and climbed the next flight of stairs, not creakily now, but in horribly fast, springy leaps like a ninja warrior. Its head whipped round, peering here, there, super-alert to its surroundings.

It wouldn't be long before it cornered its quarry. Avenger put a wooden hand up to its ear jewellery, the strange bone tube that Jin had spotted. But, no, it wasn't time to use it yet. Not until it was looking Mizz Z right in the eye.

Down in the main hall, Dad and Jin were blundering about.

'Where'd they go?' said Dad, puzzled.

Then Jin remembered. 'Frankie said they came up some stairs from the cellar. Maybe they went back that way. It's through that swing door we hid behind.'

So Jin and Dad rushed down there and checked. But there was no one at all in the cellars. They were silent as tombs. And the bakery was shut up and dark and empty. There were no signs at all that two fleeing people being pursued by a deadly tracker had passed that way.

So they'd gone back to the main hall to start again.

'We're wasting time! It's going to kill Mizz Z!' raved Jin, falling over the pharaoh's golden toilet. He bounced back up straight-away, just like he always did.

But, for once, he was angry at himself. 'You twit!' he said, smacking his forehead. When he panicked he always got extra clumsy. But he just couldn't help it – he was so scared for Frankie and Mizz Z, so freaked out by Avenger.

It was Dad who calmed him down. 'Look for clues,' he urged him. 'Like I do when I'm rat-tracking. Get focused. Empty your mind of everything else.'

'What am I supposed to look for?' said Jin.

'Anything,' said Dad. 'Any tiny sign that'll tell us where they went.'

Jin shut his eyes, breathed deeply and opened them again. *Look for signs*, he ordered himself. *Focus*. And suddenly he found himself back in control. His mind felt sharp, his worries stopped their deafening clamour. He walked around, his keen eyes searching.

What's that? he thought. He squatted down, licked his finger and picked up what he'd seen on the tip. It was a shiny black sequin. 'Hey, Dad!' he called.

Dad came striding over.

'It's from Frankie's dress,' said Jin. 'I remember her sewing them on. She said silver ones were too cheerful.'

'Good find!' said Dad. 'Where was it?'

'On the first step of those stairs going up.'

Dad peered up the stairs. Something was sparkling on a higher step, a tiny black star in the gloom. 'There's another,' he said. 'This must be the way they went. Look at this.'

Jin inspected the marks on the wall. There were fresh scrapes in the paint, like long gashes. Dad rubbed some of the paint flakes between his thumb and finger.

'See,' he said to Jin. The smear on his thumb was a mixture of white and gritty brown.

'Avenger,' whispered Jin, feeling his heart cramp with dread. 'It must be.' As it climbed, its rusty spikes had gouged the white paint off the wall.

Dad nodded, his face grave. 'It's *definitely* on their trail. And I'll tell you one thing. That thing can track. Did you see how it sniffed Mizz Z's headwrap back there?'

But Jin was already rushing up the stairs.

Frankie and Mizz Z had almost reached the roof. The last flight of steps was the narrowest, the most twisty and badly lit. As they climbed through the gloom, Mizz Z had her mobile jammed to her ear.

'What're you doing?' panted Frankie. 'This is no time to make phone calls. That wooden porcupine might catch us up.'

'I'm ringing my father in Africa,' Mizz Z calmly informed her, 'but he's not answering.' She spoke rapidly into the phone in Chewa. 'I have left him a message,' she told Frankie. 'I want to know why the Crocodile King hates us Zauyamakandas. Why he has put this curse on us.'

'But what if your dad doesn't know?' asked Frankie.

'Then he will find out,' said Mizz Z. 'My dad is a most resourceful man.' She slid her phone back into her pocket.

Frankie stopped – one last door to go. She stared at it in disbelief. 'It's a new door!' she cried, appalled. 'The old one had a bolt you slid back, then you just walked out onto the roof.'

The new door warned, in big red letters: ONLY OPEN IN AN EMERGENCY. THIS FIRE DOOR IS ALARMED.

Frankie said, 'If we open it, all hell will break loose.'

Mizz Z tutted. 'There is no need for bad language. Is there another way up to the roof?'

'I don't know!' was Frankie's frantic answer.

But then Mizz Z said, 'Did you hear that?'

Frankie listened, her face screwed up. Then she heard it – a rasping of metal, the rapid, relentless rhythm of footsteps on wood, *clack, clack, clack, clack*.

'Avenger's coming,' whispered Mizz Z. 'It's moving very quickly.'

'Quickly?' repeated Frankie.

'Yes,' nodded Mizz Z, with amazing self-composure. 'I fear we have lost our advantage.'

Frankie froze, as if an icy hand squeezed her heart.

It was Mizz Z who sprang into action.

Shoving past Frankie, she pushed up the safety bar to open the fire door. Straight away a shrieking alarm spread through the building and Mizz Z dragged Frankie out onto the museum's flat roof.

Stars peppered the dark sky above them. Chinatown was just below them. Beyond that, the city spread out, a haze of twinkling lights with the wide river snaking through it. But they had no time to admire the view.

'Where's the way down?' said Mizz Z urgently. 'Come on, girl,' she said, giving Frankie a shake. 'Tell me. Or we'll be trapped up here with Avenger.'

'There's a fire escape,' Frankie burst out, suddenly finding her voice. With the night wind tugging her hair, she flew to the roof edge. For one panic-filled moment she thought, *What if they've changed that too?* She peered down. 'Over here!' she cried out.

Mizz Z strode to join her. Even in her hurry, she could see Frankie's tag. It was faded but still there, sprayed on an old chimneypot –

that tiny red Chinese dragon, breathing a fiery capital 'F'.

Mizz Z shook her head. 'Like a wild dog peeing,' she murmured to herself, not unkindly.

While Frankie and Mizz Z were clanging down the metal fire escape on the outside of the museum, inside, Jin and Dad had stopped climbing upwards.

They stood on a landing beside a long window, the alarm screaming hysterically all around them.

'What do we do now?' bawled Jin into Dad's ear.

But then, before their astonished eyes, Frankie's biker boots appeared *outside* the window, followed by Frankie herself, her clothes blacker than the black night sky. Now Mizz Z was on the fire escape. The jazzy colours of her outfit were lost in shadows, but there was no mistaking that tall, willowy figure. Then she, too, was gone.

'Hi!' yelled Jin. The window wouldn't

open, so he hammered on the glass. But it was far too late.

'They didn't even see us,' said Jin, dismayed.

Dad jabbed his thumb downwards. 'Come on,' he mouthed. And through the shrieking din they hurried back towards the ground floor.

Meanwhile, Avenger had reached the roof of the museum. It squatted on the parapet, twisting its neck this way and that, like a snake about to strike.

Time hadn't been kind to Avenger. Passed from one careless owner to another, it had been rusted, battered, knocked about. As Frankie said, you could mistake it for a heap of junk. You might have thrown it in a skip.

But that was before it got activated and regained its ancient powers. Anyone trying that now was in for a very nasty shock.

Avenger unwound the net from its waist. It was made of fine silky mesh that could be scrunched up really small. It folded the net in its wooden hand and gazed downwards. The darkness didn't bother the ancient tracker as its eyes could see just as well at night as in daylight. It could track you by sight, sound or smell. As it got closer, it knew when you sweated from fear, or your heartbeat quickened from running. Or if your breathing grew slow and steady when you lay down to sleep, exhausted, thinking you'd escaped.

Mizz Z and Frankie arrived, breathless, at the bottom of the fire escape.

'Is Avenger following?' said Mizz Z, staring upwards. The fire escape zigzagged down the side of the museum, its iron ladders glimmering in the moonlight. They were empty.

Then Frankie pointed a trembling hand. 'It's up there!' she said.

A shape was hunched on the very edge of the roof, like some sinister bird of prey. Even from here they could see its eyes, twin golden beams piercing the dark.

'Why didn't it follow us?' asked Frankie. 'Maybe it's given up the chase.'

'Don't kid yourself,' said Mizz Z briskly. 'I have to keep running.'

'You mean *we* do,' said Frankie.

Mizz Z turned and stared at Frankie with that fierce tiger eye. 'Frankie,' she said, 'why are you doing this? We have not known each other that long. We are not related. You don't owe me this kind of loyalty.'

Frankie met Mizz Z's gaze with angry defiance. 'I just want to stay, right?'

Frankie didn't do flattery. She wasn't going to tell Mizz Z how much she admired and trusted her – because Mizz Z was cool and wise and courageous. And because Mizz Z, during their last adventure, had been able to crack through that tough, prickly shell Frankie protected herself with and find the softer Frankie inside.

So she just muttered, 'I want to stay with you and you can't stop me.'

'We'll see about that,' said Mizz Z.

Inside the museum, the alarms were still screaming. Suddenly another sound added to the chaos – the wailing of police cars, getting louder, heading in their direction. 'I bet they're coming here,' said Frankie. 'We'd better move.'

Mizz Z walked a few quick steps and peered through the red pillars of the Friendship Arch. She saw that the bakery was closed and dark, though smoke suddenly puffed up through the pavement grille. It must be from the mighty Iron Dragon. The bun-steaming stove, Mizz Z recalled, never slept. It was kept alight night and day.

Then Mizz Z spotted a man lurking in the shadows, outside the Money Tree bakery.

'Who's that?' she hissed to Frankie, now right beside her.

'It's Mr Lu,' Frankie whispered back. 'He owns the bakery down the street.'

Mr Lu was gazing jealously at the ancient money tree in its blue and white pot. He was thinking: *What if the Tangs' lucky tree mysteriously went missing? I should like to see their faces!*

Mizz Z had no idea of the plan that Lu was hatching. She dismissed him as some harmless guy out for a stroll. Her gaze swept past him and the Money Tree bakery to the main street beyond. It was still lit up and lively, bustling with happy families visiting restaurants.

'I can't go that way,' she decided. 'Too many people.'

Frankie said, 'Didn't you hear? I just said *we* have to keep running.'

Mizz Z frowned. She turned and confronted Frankie. 'You must go. You and Jin and your dad must stay right away from me. It is me Avenger is pursuing. I'm not sure why. But I am the cursed person. You are not.'

'No chance,' said Frankie, with that stubborn tilt of her chin. 'Wherever you go, I go.'

Mizz Z said, 'I am ordering you, Frankie!'

'It's still no,' said Frankie, snapping her mouth shut like a turtle. Then she opened it again and added, 'And don't start all that hero stuff – "I alone must take the risks."'

Suddenly Mizz Z's fierce gaze melted. The

ghost of a smile escaped her lips: 'Sometimes, Frankie, you are a very annoying person.'

'Not like you, then,' said Frankie, grinning back.

'I suppose I am stuck with you,' Mizz Z accepted. 'For the moment. But when I say go again, you go. Is that understood?'

Frankie put her head on one side and gazed at Mizz Z with an innocent, wide-eyed stare.

'*Is that understood, Frankie?*'

'Oh, yeah, absolutely,' Frankie replied.

'In the meantime,' said Mizz Z, 'we need a place to hide out where there are no people. The public must not be put in danger. That is RAAAA's golden rule.'

'But won't Avenger just follow you wherever you go?' said Frankie. 'You said no one the Croc King curses *ever* escapes.' She glanced upwards. But Avenger was still way above them, perched on the parapet.

'That is correct,' agreed Mizz Z. 'But I need time to work out a plan.'

Frankie nodded. She tried to search her

scrambled brain. 'I can't think,' she said in despair. 'I can't think of a place to hide.'

'Let's keep moving,' said Mizz Z. 'You can think on the way.'

Suddenly a voice shouted from the museum's second storey. On their way back down, Jin had found a window that opened. He stuck his head out, with the siren shrieking in the background. 'Why's this alarm going off?'

'We did it!' screamed Frankie.

Jin was about to yell a second question, 'Where's Avenger?' But Frankie had already turned to run. So instead Jin bawled, 'Wait for me!'

'Frankie!' Dad yelled, pushing Jin aside. 'Wait right there! We're coming down!'

But Mizz Z ordered, in her sternest tones, 'Don't follow! It is far too dangerous! Go straight home! Both of you!'

Jin watched Mizz Z and his big sister racing off, away from Chinatown.

'Think I'm going a bit deaf,' Jin murmured as he slammed the window closed. ''Cos I never heard what Mizz Z just said about going straight home.'

As Mizz Z and Frankie plunged into an alley, police cars came wailing into the museum car park, blue lights flashing. Policemen and women leaped out and pounded in heavy boots towards the building.

Up on the rooftop Avenger wasn't concerned with any of this. The mayhem below was a minor distraction. All its ancient powers were focused on one thing – tracking down Mizz Z and terminating her as the Crocodile King's curse decreed. Its glowing eyes cut through darkness. Mizz Z thought she was invisible down in the alleyways. But not from Avenger's all-seeing eyes.

Frankie suddenly yelled, 'Wait!'

Mizz Z skidded to a stop among the overflowing wheelie bins.

'I know where we'll go,' panted Frankie. 'We'll go to the City Farm. It's down by the river.'

'There are no people there?' enquired Mizz Z.

'Not at this time of night,' said Frankie.

'An excellent idea,' said Mizz Z. 'And can we go all the way to this place through these passageways?'

'Practically,' answered Frankie. The old part of the city was a maze of alleys and steps that squeezed between buildings, right down to the river. Frankie knew all these short cuts by heart.

Wild cheering came from Mizz Z's pocket. She pulled out her mobile and answered it. In seconds, she was engaged in deep conversation, in Chewa, with whoever was calling.

Then Frankie had another idea. She glanced at Mizz Z but the inspector had her back turned away, busy talking in low, urgent tones.

Frankie took her red spray can out of her pocket. Mizz Z had forbidden Jin to follow. She'd told him to go home. But Frankie knew he wouldn't. She had a lot of respect for her little brother. He almost never let things defeat him, and he'd rush in to help, whatever the odds.

If I know you, bro', thought Frankie, *you're right behind us.*

Secretly, so Mizz Z couldn't see, she started spraying her dragon tag and leaving a trail to make it easier for Jin to follow.

Avenger watched its quarry getting further and further away until it seemed that the statue, even with its newly greased joints, could never catch up. It would have to climb down four storeys to ground level, then pursue Mizz Z through many twisty back streets.

No, it wouldn't. Avenger looked down at the crowded rooftops of Chinatown. It stood up, catching the moonlight. Frankie had called it a scrapyard statue, but for a moment the oiled metal on its body flashed and glittered until it seemed like part of the starry constellations.

In one incredible leap it sprang onto the roof of the Money Tree bakery. As it flew through the dark, the net gripped in its hand unfurled and spread out behind it like a silver cloud.

Avenger landed lightly on the tiles. It folded its net again into a small package in its wooden palm. Then, like the best free runner anywhere in the world, ever, it took off again, sprinting over roofs, leaping from building to building, tracking Mizz Z across the city skyline.

Chapter Nine

As Dad and Jin slipped out of the side door of the museum, police were hammering on the main doors.

'I'll just go and tell those guys about Doctor Cramp,' said Dad. 'He didn't look too clever. He might need a hospital check-up.'

'There isn't time,' said Jin wildly. 'Come on, Dad! We got to find some way to stop that Avenger thing.'

And Jin ran ahead, to the alley where he'd seen Frankie and Mizz Z disappear. He thought that, with his slow, shambolic running style, he'd never catch up. But tonight his feet seemed to have wings. He flew through the shadows of that long, twisty alley, dodging the wheelie bins.

Behind him, Dad took a quick glance at the police. They'd found the side door and were pouring into the building, looking for robbers. Seconds later the alarm stopped.

They'll soon find the curator, Dad reassured himself. Then he yelled, 'Wait for me, Jin.' And set out after his son.

A burning pain in his ribs stopped Jin in his tracks. He bent double, whooping for air. He'd never run so fast. 'Hey, speedy dude,' he congratulated himself, 'you only bumped into one wheelie bin!' For him, that was a big achievement. But Jin had noticed before that since Mizz Z had crashed like a fiery comet into his life, he'd achieved some pretty amazing things. Things he'd never thought he was capable of. It was like she'd given his mind a big shake-up; made him expect more of himself.

He couldn't think about this now; he was on a mission. *Where'd they go?* he wondered, straightening up as the pain in his side eased. He'd arrived at a T-junction. Should he go to

the right or the left? For a moment Jin almost panicked. He was no good at all with directions. His head turned one way, then the other. 'You've lost them!' he raged at himself. He slammed his palm into his forehead in despair.

And to make things worse, a mist was rolling in from the river, sneaking up the alleyways like grey smoke.

But then Jin heard Dad's voice in his head: *Find a trail. Look for signs.* 'Like sequins,' he told himself, calming down.

He took the right-hand turn, squinting through the gloom, trying to spot one of those tiny, sparkling dots. He didn't see any at all, even though he crawled on all fours, under the mist, his nose close to the cobblestones. He went to the left. He didn't find any sequins there, either. But he found something much better. Frankie had sprayed her tag on the inside of a thrown-away pizza box. She'd left it propped against the alley wall, like a picture in an art gallery.

Jin squatted down, reached out a hand and touched the fierce little dragon. Frankie could paint him in four seconds, with just a few quick swoops of her spray can. Jin's finger came away with a blood-red tip. The paint hadn't even dried yet.

'Good old Frankie,' he murmured.

He leaped to his feet, hope fizzing again inside him, and hurried along the alley, thinking, *They can't be far away*. He kept his eyes peeled, looking out for the next dragon sign. He even yelled ahead into the dark: 'Frankie! Mizz Z!'

From somewhere high above him, he heard a faint, tinny, rasping noise. He skidded to a stop and stared upwards, his eyes searching. Then he heard a whooshing sound and a soft thud. Jin's head whipped round.

'Avenger!' he breathed, his blood chilling. The spiky wooden statue was behind him, in a panther crouch. Where had it come from? It seemed to have dropped from the sky.

Avenger straightened up, standing in a pool

of moonlight that was spilling into the alley. Because of the mist, it couldn't track Mizz Z any more from the rooftops. So it had come back to ground level to hunt her down.

Avenger was the same height as Jin, their eyes on a level. And Jin found himself gazing into two glowing discs. There was no expression in them at all. They were as blank as an amber traffic light.

Instinctively Jin knew not to run. It would chase him, like a greyhound does a rabbit. He'd already noticed that it seemed much more athletic than before. Jin had run faster just now than he'd ever run in his life, but if it came to a race between him and Avenger, Jin knew he stood no chance.

The ancient wooden statue and the human boy stood staring at each other. Very slowly Jin started backing away. But then his quick eyes detected a movement. Something was unfolding, like a blossoming flower, from Avenger's right hand.

Just as his panicking brain was thinking,

What's that? a familiar voice bawled, 'Jin! Move! Now!'

Jin fell, rather than leaped, out of the way as the net came whirling through the air and landed, in shimmering folds, exactly where he had been standing.

Then Avenger was loping towards him. It stretched out a hand, like a spiky gauntlet. Jin yelled out, 'Gerroff me!' He curled himself up, his arms protecting his head. Rolled up like a hedgehog, Jin's blood was roaring in his ears; there was a dancing red mist in his brain. Then he felt himself being yanked to his feet. 'Gerroff!' he yelled again, his legs kicking out wildly.

'It's me, Jin. It's me. Open your eyes.'

Jin realized his eyes were screwed shut. He opened them. And there was Dad, looking anxiously into his face.

'It's OK,' said Dad. 'It's gone.'

Jin couldn't believe it. His legs felt so weak and shaky that he had to hang onto a wheelie bin so he didn't fall down.

'What happened?' he asked.

'It just picked up its net and sprinted off. Cool as anything.'

'I thought it was coming to get me.'

Mr Sparks said, 'Soon as you got out of its way, it ignored you. Mizz Z is the one it's after. See how it threw that net? That's amazing. I mean, I've got a rat-catching net' – Dad pointed to a small leather pouch on his belt – 'and the guys say I'm a good shot. But that Avenger, it's in a different league. If that's a machine, it's more advanced than any modern robot . . .' He was lost for words. He could only shake his head in admiration.

'Anyway, thanks, Dad,' said Jin. 'I mean, really, thanks a lot. If you hadn't turned up when you did and shouted, if I hadn't moved . . .' He didn't finish the sentence. But he imagined himself struggling like a fish in the net's silvery meshes, getting more and more entangled as Avenger approached. 'What would it have done, Dad?' he wondered, his eyes wide and haunted. 'I mean, if I hadn't moved out its way? If it had trapped me in that net? How would it have finished me off? Mizz Z told Frankie that no one ever survived. Not people who'd been cursed, or people that got in its way. Frankie said they died of—'

But before Jin could say 'terror', Dad interrupted. 'No time to think of that now,' he told Jin. He hadn't been convinced before that Avenger was really dangerous. But now he'd seen it in action, he had no doubts at all. 'We've got to keep moving,' he muttered, frowning. 'We mustn't let it get too far ahead.' He marched off down the alley and disappeared into the misty dark.

Jin felt something flapping on his nose. It was the skull plaster. In all the mayhem, it had come unstuck. Jin pressed it firmly back on again. Then, his face fierce and determined, he went striding after his dad.

'Dad, did you see Frankie's tag?' he gasped, when he caught up.

'Yeah.' Dad nodded.

'There it is again,' said Jin, pointing to a

little red dragon freshly sprayed on a dumped mattress with the springs bursting out.

'Smart girl,' said Dad. 'She's left us a trail.'

Together, they followed the dragon trail to the end of the alley. A sudden wind had got up. It came gusting past them, blowing the mist away.

'Where now?' asked Dad, squinting through the shadows. Two alleys snaked off from this one. 'We'll just have to search for more of Frankie's tags,' he said.

But then Jin spotted something on the top of a wall. It was Frankie's spray can. It seemed she'd left it there deliberately for them to find. He picked it up, shook it. 'It's empty,' he told Dad. 'She's run out of paint.' There wouldn't be any more little red dragons to show them the way. 'We've lost them again,' he said.

'No, we haven't,' said Dad. 'Look here.' His voice sounded strong and confident. He was down one of the alleyways, staring at a tough little weed sprouting between the bricks of a wall.

'Remember,' said Dad, when Jin joined him, 'that I told you that rats have greasy fur? That they leave marks wherever they go? Well, look at this plant.'

For a second Jin was bewildered. He thought Dad had lost the plot. 'But we're not tracking rats!' he protested.

'It wasn't a rat that left this. It was Avenger.'

Jin thought of the grease glistening on Avenger's wooden body, even on its metal Mohawk. That grease would be bound to leave traces, wherever it went. 'But how do you know it's Avenger?' asked Jin. 'And not some scabby old city rat?'

'Smell,' said Dad, tearing off a greasy leaf and sticking it under Jin's nose. Jin caught a stale, meaty stink.

'That's *definitely* not rat smell,' explained Dad. 'It's something else – whatever Avenger used to grease its joints. Anyway, we've picked up the trail again.'

Jin and Dad hurried along the alley, their

sharp eyes flicking everywhere, searching for more grease marks. At the same time, random thoughts flashed through Jin's mind, like they always did in times of crisis. One was, *It's dead lucky Dad's a rat-catcher.* Without Dad's tracking skills they'd have lost the trail long ago. And another was, *Hey, I'm not bad at this tracking business, either.* Jin would have smiled at this discovery if he hadn't been so scared and upset. Because it was yet another talent that he had no idea he had.

'There's one,' he said, spotting an oily smear on a brick. He crouched, put his nose close and sniffed, using his senses like a good tracker should. Then, in a strong, confident voice, he told Dad, 'That's Avenger grease, no doubt about it.'

In the little room at the City Museum, Dr Cramp had slowly come back to his senses, after the terrible trauma of having the Crocodile King's spirit take over his mind and body. The curator heard, as if in a dream, alarms going off, wailing sirens. Now different sounds penetrated his brain – the din of fists hammering on doors, people bellowing: 'Police! Open up!'

'I'm coming, I'm coming!' groaned the doctor, standing up shakily and staggering past the baobab tree.

The king's empty mask was still on the floor, where Mizz Z had left it. The curator glanced at the palm-leaf fronds, spread out like a giant fan, and at the wooden head with its gaping croc jaws and cruel fangs.

He gave a great shudder, turned his eyes away and stumbled out of the little room. Jin had been right. The curator had learned his lesson not to mess with the Crocodile King. There was no way he was going to get inside that mask ever again.

But someone else would . . .

The African Giant Pouched Rat trundled into the little room, still searching for a place to hide. It had splinters of blue and white china in its fur, from when the toilet bowl had shattered around it.

It sniffed at the crocodile mask, its long whiskers trembling. It peered through the snaggle-toothed jaws.

'*Eeek! Eeek!*' it squeaked in excitement. That looked like a cosy nest! Like any rat, it loved deep, dark holes where it could feel safe.

It crept into the crocodile mask and snuggled down.

Suddenly from inside the baobab came a rattling and thumping. Something seemed to be stirring.

The Crocodile King, now he'd had a taste of his old power, was hungrier than ever to become flesh and blood again. And he sensed something warm and alive inside his old mask, a creature with a beating heart and a brain.

The door to the baobab burst open. The air began to shiver. The shivers spread out towards the mask like ripples on a pond . . .

There was the sudden clatter of boots.

The police were coming this way. The Giant Pouched Rat could feel the floor vibrating.

'*Eeek! Eeek!*'

It shot out of the crocodile mask, back into the main hall. Seconds later, police officers came crashing through the doors. The Giant Pouched Rat scuttled behind the pharaoh's golden toilet.

In the small room, the ripples whisked back into the baobab, like a genie trapped again in its bottle. Then the door of the spirit tree slammed shut.

Chapter Ten

Frankie said, 'We're here.'

Mizz Z's amber eye took a quick scope around the City Farm.

It was a tiny place, down by the river, tucked away under a railway viaduct.

'Not many people even know there's a farm here,' Frankie informed Mizz Z.

During the day, a glossy black cockerel strutted about with his hens scratching and clucking around him. There were some pigs, a few sheep, even two horses for city kids to ride. But now the whole place was silent and plunged into shadow. The pens were empty and the animals all safely shut away in hen-houses, sties and stables.

The only sound came from the river, just a

few metres away. The tide was coming in and you could hear the *slop, slop* of waves as they washed over the mud banks.

Suddenly there was a rattling din above them. Mizz Z thought, *Avenger!* But it was only a red and yellow metro train, its windows bright squares of light, rocking across the viaduct into the city.

Is the metro still running? thought Frankie, surprised. She checked her watch. It was midnight. *Is that all?* Only three hours had passed since she'd been selling custard tarts at the Money Tree bakery, but it seemed like a lifetime ago.

'Can we get inside?' asked Mizz Z, looking at the triple-padlocked main gates and the high wire fence all around the farm.

'Course,' shrugged Frankie. 'There's another gate, into the sheep pen, that you can climb over.'

Mizz Z nodded. 'Let us do that, then,' she said casually, as if she was out for a walk in the park. Not being tracked by a deadly ancient artefact that wouldn't stop until she'd been terminated.

'Watch out, it's a bit mucky,' Frankie instructed, climbing over the gate into the sheep pen.

'"A bit mucky",' said Mizz Z tersely. 'That is an understatement. It is a good job my flip-flops have platform soles.' She didn't ask whether Frankie had climbed into the farm before at night – she knew Frankie had a secret life, and that she didn't appreciate being questioned about it. She picked her way across the pen to the shed where the sheep were kept. She drew back the bolts and opened the door wide. Four confused sheep and two lambs on wobbly legs came baaing out into the moonlight. They crowded around Frankie and Mizz Z, thinking it was feed-ing time.

'What did you let them out for?' hissed Frankie.

'I'm trying to buy us some time,' said Mizz Z, 'while I plan my next move. All these animal smells might throw Avenger off the scent.'

Avenger was quite close. But it was still in the dark maze of alleyways. It bent its crested head and sniffed at the shred of headwrap. It lifted its ancient face, battered like a prize fighter's, as if smelling the air. But Mizz Z's fragrant hair oil was swamped by the animal smells from the City Farm.

No matter. Avenger had many different ways to track its human prey. It dropped to one knee, its eyes, sharp as a hawk's, searching the ground for footprints or other signs.

A lamb was nibbling a black frill that draggled from Frankie's frock. She stroked its soft, woolly head. 'Was that your dad on the phone before?' she asked Mizz Z. 'What did he say?'

'There's no time for details,' said Mizz Z. 'But here is what my father found out. We Zauyamakandas spoke up fearlessly against the Crocodile King. We didn't like his cruelty or his injustice. I am talking about hundreds of years ago now, in the olden days, when the king was alive. So, naturally, we became his enemies. He vowed to wipe us from the face of the earth.'

'That's terrible!' Frankie burst out, scaring the lamb, who skipped back to its mother.

'But the king never got the chance,' Mizz Z continued. 'He died. Of eating too many unripe mangoes – he was a very greedy man. And soon after his death his mask and Avenger were stolen, so the king's spirit stayed trapped in the old baobab tree. Until, of course, it took over Doctor Cramp's body. But it seems the king never forgot his hatred of us Zauya-makandas. Because as soon as he found out my name, he cursed me and the rest of my family. And sent Avenger to hunt us down.'

'Did your dad hear all this from a story-teller in your village?' asked Frankie.

'No, he searched the Net. Everything is online these days! He found an old, forgotten book about African legends. A book even I,' confessed Mizz Z, 'with my vast knowledge, have never come across. I should have known this already.'

'Should have known what?' asked Frankie.

'About my family, the Zauyamakandas. That they were once heroes. That they stood up to a tyrant.'

Frankie shrugged. 'I don't know much about my family. I've got loads of Chinese aunties I've never met.'

But Mizz Z didn't seem to hear her.

'It's so strange,' she mused, as if speaking to herself. 'I am an expert on ancient arte-facts from all over the world, but I know so little about my own family. My grandmother probably knew. I always meant to ask her more about the Crocodile King, but I never did. And then she started to forget her old stories. And it was too late.'

Mizz Z's mind flashed back to her home village and Granny Zauyamakanda sitting out-side her house sipping a beer and smoking her long clay pipe after a hard day's work in her vegetable garden, telling her stories to anyone who would listen.

I did listen sometimes, she thought. *When I had nothing better to do.*

Mizz Z frowned. She needed to keep her brain clear. This was no time to cloud it with regrets. It was just that, when Avenger was hunting you down, when by dawn you might be dead, it tended to focus your mind on things that were truly important.

'There was some more information in this same book,' Mizz Z told Frankie. 'It was about Avenger.'

'Oh, yeah?' said Frankie, her skin crawling. 'Do I want to hear this?'

'Probably not,' said Mizz Z. 'The book also tells us that Avenger didn't kill those the king cursed.'

'But that's great news!' Frankie burst out. 'I thought you—'

'Wait!' Mizz Z interrupted her, grim-faced. 'Avenger's method was this. It tracked you down. It netted you so you were helpless.

Then it sent for something else more frightening – some other thing that made people die of terror.'

'What *other thing*?' echoed Frankie, aghast. 'What could be more frightening than Avenger?'

'The book doesn't say,' Mizz Z told her. 'I suppose because no one survived. They found one poor man before he died and he kept mumbling one word. "*Darkness*",' he said. "*Darkness*".'

'That's not much help, is it?' Frankie protested. 'Didn't he say anything else?'

Suddenly something spooked the horses, shut up inside their stable. Frankie could hear them kicking at their stalls, snorting and whinnying.

Is it Avenger? she wondered, her eyes wide with dread. She felt her heart give a sick jolt, then rev up and start to race.

Mizz Z caught Frankie's panic. She stared nervously around. But she couldn't see any movement out there in the dark. *Get a grip,*

A. J. Zauyamakanda, she told herself, ruth-lessly crushing her fear.

In the alleyways, Avenger's eyes sparked once, twice, like yellow fire. For the first time it could detect not just Frankie's fear, but the fear of Mizz Z, the Crocodile King's accursed enemy. She had only given way to it for a few seconds. But that was long enough for Avenger to sense her fast-beating heart, the blood pulsing through her veins.

Now it knew exactly where she was. It took off towards the City Farm in a long, loping sprint. It was quite aware that, behind it, Jin and his dad were on its trail, painstakingly searching for the grease marks it had left. But it also knew they were of no account. They had no powers to stop it. No human ever had.

At the City Farm, Frankie grabbed Mizz Z's arm. She said feverishly, 'Come on, let's go.'

'No,' Mizz Z suddenly declared, with a flash of her amber eye. 'I have made a decision. I *refuse* to keep running for the rest of my life. I will go back to the museum. There I will defeat the Crocodile King and end the curse on my family.'

'But how?' asked Frankie.

Mizz Z said mysteriously, 'I shall ring RAAAA's secret HQ here in UK. I'll get them to rush me some help.'

'Why didn't you do that before?' said Frankie. But she already knew the answer. The proud Mizz Z liked to fix things alone. She hated to admit she needed help on a mission.

Mizz Z was already speaking to RAAAA. She gave many instructions in a low, urgent voice. The only words Frankie caught clearly were 'Crocodile Stones'. Mizz Z repeated this several times.

When Mizz Z ended her call, Frankie's mouth opened to ask, 'What are these Crocodile Stones?'

But the Chief Inspector got in first. 'You can't come with me,' she told Frankie. 'From now on, I alone must run the risks. Avenger will follow me back to the museum. It won't harm you if you keep out of its way.'

Frankie opened her mouth to protest, but Mizz Z stopped her. 'We *agreed* you should go when I said,' she reminded Frankie sternly. 'Are you now going to break your word?'

'No,' said Frankie. She didn't want to confess it, even to herself, but she was relieved to be ordered to leave. She'd meant to be so strong and brave. But she couldn't stand this nightmare a moment longer.

Then Mizz Z held up her hand and said, 'Listen!'

All the animals on the City Farm seemed suddenly restless. Frantic squawking came from inside the henhouse, squeals from the pigs. Even the sheep huddled around the lambs, protecting them, as if they sensed something dreadful coming this way.

Mizz Z went to the gate of the sheep pen. She gazed into the shadows. *Nothing*, she thought.

And then she saw them – two pinpricks

of yellow light in the distant darkness, getting bigger as they came this way. The nerve below her eye patch twitched madly. But her voice, when she spoke to Frankie, was steady.

'Stay in the sheep pen,' she commanded. 'I will lead it away from here. Wait until it has followed me, then go straight home.'

'OK,' said Frankie, for once not arguing. Then she added, 'Mizz Z, will you be all right?'

Mizz Z was climbing out of the sheep pen. She looked back and saw Frankie's anguished face. She switched on her bravest, most brilliant smile. 'Hey, cheer up, girl,' she commanded Frankie. 'It is not the end of the world. I will be fine.' Then with a breezy wave of her hand she said, 'See you later!' and disappeared into the dark.

Frankie stood alone, waiting. She was shaking so much the last few sequins fell from her dress. She started to chew her nails. The sheep were stampeding around the pen, pushing, shoving, as if trying to escape from a pack of wolves.

Frankie wondered where Jin and Dad had got to.

Please, please, she thought, *don't let them get in Avenger's way*.

Then suddenly, with a mighty grasshopper spring, one of the panicking lambs leaped right over the gate.

'No!' yelled Frankie, far too late.

The lamb landed on the path between the City Farm and the river. It didn't scoot off but just stayed there, trembling and bleating pathetically for its mum.

Frankie stopped thinking. She just dived for the gate, clambered madly over it and scooped up the lamb.

She straightened. And saw two glowing discs staring straight at her. It was Avenger, the best tracking machine in the world, ever. It was hot on the trail of Mizz Z. And Frankie was in its way.

Move! Frankie's brain screamed at her. But

she couldn't – she was helpless, frozen to the spot. The lamb wriggled from her arms and squeezed back through the bars of the gate. But Frankie hardly noticed.

She couldn't take her eyes off Avenger's face. As if in a dream, she saw its lips pulled back in a snarl, showing two rows of needle-sharp teeth; its nose, as bashed about as a boxer's; its round eyes, empty as a killer shark's. And its metal Mohawk that gleamed in the moonlight, like the helmet crest of some ancient warrior.

Then Frankie heard a soft *chink, chink*. The sound seemed to shock her out of her trance.

Her gaze shot down to Avenger's right hand. The back of its hand, like the rest of its body, bristled with sharp, spiky metal. And Frankie saw that its wooden fingers were slowly opening, so its net could unfurl.

She took off, running in a blind panic, anywhere, just to get away from Avenger. She stumbled down the bank to the river, climbing over some fly-tipped rubbish. She tried to run away across the mud flats. But it felt like her feet were stuck in wet cement. She struggled a few more steps.

Slurp, slurp. As she pulled out her biker boot, the mud made horrible gobbling sounds. She put her foot down again. Instantly the mud gulped it up. This time, when she tried to tug it free, the mud wouldn't let go.

Frankie tugged again. Now both her feet were trapped. 'Arrgh!' She gave a scream of rage and despair. Then she felt something cold slopping around her legs and she looked down. It was greasy, grey river water.

Up on the bank, Avenger slotted that thin yellow tube back into its right ear lobe. It wasn't a piece of jewellery, as Jin had thought when he'd first spotted it. It was a bone whistle. After Avenger had flicked out its net, lightning-fast, and ensnared its victim, it would blow the whistle to summon the final terror.

But this time, that wasn't needed. It didn't even have to throw its net. Its victim was already doomed, stuck fast out on the wide, empty mud flats, with the tide coming in.

Avenger scrunched the net back into its palm. It turned its glowing eyes in the direction Mizz Z had taken and loped off into the dark.

Chapter Eleven

Frankie wasn't far from the river bank. But there was no way she could reach it. She couldn't see it, either. Clouds had slid over the moon and it was suddenly pitch black out on the mud flats.

She shrieked through the dark, 'Help me!'

She tried again to pull her legs free. But that wasn't a good idea. She wobbled sickeningly, and almost sprawled face down in the slimy mud. Then, horrified, she realized something else.

'I'm sinking,' she whispered. Every time she struggled the mud sucked her further in. Now she couldn't even see her biker boots. 'Keep still!' she ordered herself, using Mizz Z's commanding tones.

So she just stood there, with her heart pounding, *boom, boom, boom*, being slowly swallowed by mud that stank of rotting seaweed and dead crabs.

Suddenly a salty wind came gusting up river and whipped her long hair about. Soon the tide would be powering in from the sea and this mud flat would be three metres under-water.

'Don't look down,' Frankie told herself, half sobbing. But she had to. She saw more foamy water snaking across the mud towards her. She shrieked out again, in a voice that didn't sound like hers, that didn't even sound human, '*Help meeee!*'

In the alleyways, Jin and Dad heard that desperate scream and started running towards the City Farm.

From the river bank, Dad yelled, 'Frankie, is that you out there?'

From somewhere in the dark they heard a voice, shrill with panic, calling to them.

'That's Frankie!' said Dad.

She sounded very close. But Jin couldn't hear what she was saying. The farm animals, even though Avenger had gone, were still making a racket: whinnying, baaing, squealing and crashing about in their sheds.

Jin listened hard as Frankie yelled out again. 'She says she's stuck in the mud.'

'Where?' Dad peered into the dense blackness. 'I can't see her.'

Jin hurled himself down the grassy bank, his arms whirling like windmills to keep his balance.

'Come back!' yelled Dad. 'You'll get stuck too.'

But Jin wasn't intending to go charging out onto the mud flats. When Dad scrambled down the bank after him, he found his son squatting amongst the rubbish, using his new-found tracking skills.

'Look,' said Jin. Prints were pressed into the soft mud. Because it was so hard to see in the murky dark, he traced the shape of one with his finger. 'That's Frankie's biker boot,' he said after a few seconds. 'It must be. It's got stars on the sole, just like hers.'

'Well spotted. That's where she went onto the mud flats,' said Dad.

'You don't think Avenger followed her out there?' Jin whispered, turning to Dad, his eyes full of dread.

They both peered at the mud, trying to see. Jin leaned out and ran his hand over the smooth, wet surface. It was scribbled all over with the three-toed prints of seagulls. But there were no marks that resembled Avenger's blocky wooden feet.

Then Frankie screamed out again and the clouds parted and the mud flats were washed with a silver moonlight. Jin and Dad saw a lonely, scared figure stuck in a muddy wasteland, maybe twenty metres away from the bank.

'There she is!' said Dad. 'How'd she get out there?'

'I can't see Avenger,' said Jin, relieved.

Dad looked grim. 'It won't be hanging around here. It'll be after Mizz Z.'

Behind Frankie, choppy waves had already filled the river's main channel. Now they were spilling over and creeping across the mud flats towards her.

'I'm sinking!' she cried. 'Get me out of here!'

Jin stared at his dad in horrified disbelief. Frankie was so close, but she might have been on another planet. If they tried to go out and get her, they'd get stuck, just like her.

Dad checked his rat-fighting belt and swore under his breath. 'I've left my long rope in the van.'

Jin couldn't believe they were so helpless. *What would Mizz Z do?* She always seemed to have an answer in a crisis. He slammed his hand against his forehead. But it only shook up his scrambled brain even more. Then suddenly a scene from a film he'd once seen flashed into his mind, where some surfer kid got trapped in sinking sands. And these other kids had put their surfboards end to end and crawled out on them to rescue him.

Jin burst out, 'Dad, we need surfboards, or

something, to crawl over the mud.'

'Surfboards?' repeated Dad vaguely. But he wasn't really listening. The next second he told Jin, 'I'm going to run back to the museum car park, get that rope. Pull her out.'

Then he went striding back towards the alleyways in his big boots. He shouted over his shoulder at Jin, 'Phone the emergency services!'

'I haven't got a phone!' Jin yelled back. Dad must have forgotten. But he had already disappeared.

Jin stood staring at Frankie. He didn't know what to say. He couldn't say, 'The emergency services are on their way,' because they weren't. So he yelled, 'Dad's gone for a rope!'

Frankie's terrified eyes glowed white in the moonlight. She must have been in shock because she didn't seem to take in what he was saying. She shrieked, 'Don't just stand there!'

Jin told himself, *Do something*. But he couldn't get surfboards out of his head. Which was no use at all because he didn't have a surf-board here. He'd never even owned one. He'd always imagined that for him, surfing, with his dodgy balance, was just an impossible dream.

He looked wildly around. Amongst the dumped rubbish were giant sheets of card-board – the packing from fridge freezers. And mixed with the cardboard were great sheets of plastic foam, the same size and thickness as house doors . . .

A plan sprang, ready-made, into Jin's mind. For a moment he was stunned by its brilliance. Then immediately he was torn by doubts. What if he messed up and Dad had to rescue him as well as Frankie? He asked himself again: *What would Mizz Z do?*

And this time there was no doubt in his mind at all. Mizz Z wouldn't be standing here dithering, thinking pathetically, *What if I mess up?* She'd be sliding those plastic foam sheets out on the mud and crawling across them, just like those guys did with their surfboards. He could hear her voice in his head: *Why are you still standing there, boy? Move those bones!*

On their last adventure Mizz Z had told Jin, 'You are quite a hero.' Could she have been joking? *No*, Jin reassured himself. *She must have really meant it.* Mizz Z had many magnificent qualities. But a sense of humour wasn't among them.

Fired up with new confidence, he stopped thinking and sprang into action. He lugged the big foam sheets to the mud's edge. They were awkward to carry but light as a feather.

'I'm coming to get you, sis!' he called out. 'Stay cool.'

He slid the first one onto the mud, then used another to push it further out, then another. Until a pathway of seven plastic sheets stretched across the mud flats, gleaming white in the moonlight.

Frankie lifted her drooping head and saw what he was doing. Hope sparkled again in her eyes. She yelled encouragement to Jin. 'Come on, you can do it!'

Jin wriggled out onto the first sheet and lay

flat, hardly daring to breathe. It felt horribly insecure and bouncy, as if it were resting on jelly.

Then the plastic sheet rocked suddenly. Jin's guts twisted in panic. But it didn't sink. It just seemed to flex, like a trampoline. For a second he lay very still, making a star shape to spread his weight, his cheek resting against the cold, bubbly foam.

He decided he wasn't going to throw up. So he slithered very carefully onto the next sheet and the next, crawling commando-style, while the mud quaked beneath. *Dad could never do this*, thought Jin. *Not even Mizz Z. Only you could do it.* For this crazy journey, being a light and skinny person was a big advantage.

And there was Frankie! His sister was shivering with cold, her face streaked with mud and tears. It felt like Jin's heart had plunged down a deep dark hole. Because he saw that while he'd been crawling to get here, Frankie had sunk in the mud almost to her waist. And he knew that there was no way he could haul her out.

He still tried. He grabbed her round the waist and pulled. The plastic sheet rocked, he was almost tipped off and Frankie moved a little bit but then sank back.

'It's not working!' cried Frankie furiously. 'It's making it worse! This was a stupid idea!'

'Have you got any *better* ones!' Jin snapped back.

'I'm going to help myself! Move out of the way!'

She tried to haul herself onto the plastic foam. Jin slid backwards onto the sheet behind, while holding her sheet steady. But that didn't work, either. The mud's grip was like a vice.

For a second they stared hopelessly into each other's eyes.

'What do we do now?' Frankie asked, her voice no longer angry but small and terribly scared. Then suddenly they heard a noise like a roaring engine. She looked round, terrified. 'The water's coming!'

It came speeding over the mud flats, faster than a racehorse. Not a trickle this time, but a great rolling wave. It crashed into them and Jin heard Frankie's scream turn to gurgles.

'Frankie! Frankie!' yelled Jin. 'Where are you?'

Somehow, he was still on his board, swirling round and round. He reached down and grabbed what felt like an arm. The water had turned the mud to sloppy porridge. Suddenly it was easy to get Frankie out. When he pulled, she popped up like a cork beside him. She was choking and coughing, her hair streaming with mud and water.

'Hold onto me!' said Jin.

But then he was toppled from his sheet of plastic foam and dragged down into the brown scummy water too, spinning as if he was in a washing machine.

I'm drowning, he thought. But the next second, he saw stars and a big pale moon above him. When he opened his mouth he gulped in air, not water. Somehow, he'd burst through to the surface.

Beside him, he saw one of the plastic sheets bobbing about on the waves like a life raft. Jin heaved himself on board and looked around desperately for Frankie.

And there she was, not far away, lying face down on her own plastic sheet. 'Frankie! You all right?' he yelled urgently. He sighed with relief as the soggy heap on the raft feebly raised its head.

Frankie looked like some weird sea creature with river weed tangled in her glistening hair and tentacle frills writhing around her.

'You look terrible!' Jin shouted.

Frankie made a rude gesture, then started paddling with her hands towards the bank, and safety.

She's all right, thought Jin, grinning.

He paddled like Frankie towards the bank. The mud flats were underwater and the waves were gentle now, with that deep hush that comes at high tide. It was all very serene, with the moon reflected in the shimmering water. It felt like steering his board through the sky, trailing his hands through stars.

Hey, this is like surfing, he thought as he headed for the shore. OK, he wasn't standing up riding monster waves; he was just lying down paddling. But it was still the biggest thrill.

And for a moment, suddenly, unexpectedly, he felt a surge of pure elation. A huge soppy smile broke out all over his face.

'Surfer dude!' he whispered to himself, only half joking. He was even tempted not to head for the shore but to carry on paddling his board along the wide, gleaming river. Just to see where it took him.

Then, 'Jin! Stop messing about! Get back here, now!' Frankie yelled from the bank.

Reality came crashing back and, along with it, all the horror of the Crocodile King's curse and Mizz Z being hunted down by Avenger, that deadly tracking machine. How could he have forgotten, even for an instant? He steered his plastic sheet back to solid ground.

Frankie was sitting high up on the bank, wringing out her skirt and tipping muddy water from her biker boots. Jin scrambled to join her, his clothes dripping, his trainers squelching like a sponge.

'Bet my phone's ruined,' Frankie complained as Jin shook himself like a wet dog, spraying water drops everywhere. 'And by the way,' she muttered quickly, 'you saved my life. Thanks, bro', you're a legend.'

Jin stared at her. Frankie, being grateful? It was like Mum saying, 'Jin, don't bother about homework. Just chill out, play computer games.'

Then they heard anguished cries: 'Frankie! Frankie!'

'That's Dad, back with the rope,' said Jin.

They both staggered to their feet. 'Dad, I'm here!' Frankie called.

Mr Sparks came rushing from the shadows with the long rope slung across his chest. His face was white with shock and joy all mixed up.

'I can't believe it,' he gabbled. 'You're

alive!' He grabbed Frankie and gave her a huge squeeze. 'I thought when I saw the mud flats were flooded . . . I nearly had a heart attack . . . I thought I was too late! I was going to bring the van but it was quicker to run through the alleys . . . Look, you sure you're all right?'

'Yes, but I can't breathe,' protested Frankie as she squirmed out of her father's bear-like hug. 'I'm fine, Dad, honest, don't make a fuss. Jin rescued me.'

'You did?' said Dad, turning to Jin, amazed. 'How on earth did you do it?'

'Tell you later,' said Jin. 'There's no time now.'

'Yeah, Mizz Z's gone back to the museum,' Frankie explained, 'for some kind of show-down with the Croc King. And Avenger's right behind her. We have to get back there, right now.'

And she laced up her biker boots with an extra savage tug and took off, squelching, into the dark.

Chapter Twelve

Mizz Z was slap-slapping in her high-rise flip-flops through the dark city streets. Wild cheering came from her pocket. She skidded to a halt and answered her phone.

'Hello, RAAAA? Yes? Yes? Did you get the Crocodile Stones? What did you say? You can only send a few fragments? Why? Oh, yes, I understand. And the helicopter will be here when? Yes, I will be waiting.'

Mizz Z ended her call. But she didn't start running. Instead, she paused for a few moments. She didn't want to get too far ahead of Avenger. For once, she wasn't trying to escape the deadly tracker. She wanted to lead it on, let it know exactly where she was going. And that was a very dangerous game to play.

'But this mission *must* be done and dusted before the sun comes up,' Mizz Z murmured. She glanced at her watch. That meant she had about three hours.

If Avenger was still on the loose in daylight, members of the public would be put in danger. It was her job, as Chief Inspector, to make sure that didn't happen. And she had another, very personal, reason for wanting this mission wrapped up in the next few hours. Her little brother, Kapito, now all grown up, was flying into the city airport at six a.m. He was on a plane at this very moment, somewhere over the Atlantic Ocean. He was coming to see his big sister and do some business in the city. He had no idea about the Crocodile King, Avenger, or the curse on his family.

'You *must* win this battle, A. J. Zauyamakanda,' Mizz Z told herself grimly.

Because if she didn't, if she died trying to break the curse, the next person on Avenger's hit list would be Kapito. If Mizz Z didn't arrive at the city airport to meet him, Kapito would come looking for her. He would walk right into Avenger's net.

Mizz Z didn't often feel fear. And if she did she'd learned to hide it. But when she thought about Kapito dying, she just couldn't help it. Her proud, hawk-like features seemed to crumble. Her fierce eye clouded with pain.

Avenger, loping through the shadows, felt her terror. Its eyes flashed once, twice. It unfurled its net. But Mizz Z had spotted those twin yellow beams stabbing the darkness.

'Stay alive, A. J. Zauyamakanda,' she told herself. She took off her flip-flops and threw them away so she could run faster. Then sped off like a champion sprinter towards the City Museum.

The battle had begun.

Mizz Z raced across the City Museum car park. The police, finding no robbers, had driven away again. Despite his protests, they'd taken Dr Cramp with them for a hospital check-up. The only vehicle remaining was Mr Aaron Sparks's bright yellow council van.

Why's that still there? thought Mizz Z as she raced by. *At this time of night?* Jin, Frankie and Mr Sparks should be at home by now, out of danger.

But there was no time to worry about that. Avenger was right behind her, and at any moment RAAAA was going to deliver the pieces of Crocodile Stone.

When ancient powers were released, either deliberately or accidentally, RAAAA could swing into action with incredible speed.

Mizz Z glanced up at the stars sprinkled across the navy-blue night sky. A group of them were twinkling extra bright. They were moving, flashing on and off. They weren't stars but RAAAA's helicopter, swooping in over the city.

'Right on time,' she murmured as she raced, barefoot, up the metal steps of the fire escape to the roof of the museum.

As she was speeding upwards she glanced back across the museum car park. Avenger wasn't in sight. *Good.* Mizz Z wanted it to follow her – but she didn't want Avenger here just yet. She wanted it out of the way while she collected the stones and fought the Crocodile King. Only then could she turn her attention to stopping the deadly tracker.

But Mizz Z should have looked at the Friendship Arch.

Avenger, with its night vision, had seen her making the long, zigzag climb up the fire escape. And it had decided to take a different route. Its spiky hands and feet stabbing the wood like crampons, it was scaling the red and gold pillars that supported the arch.

Mizz Z was on the museum roof now, gazing up at the starry sky. 'Come on, come on,' she urged the copter.

It was hovering in the sky just above her. She could hear the *jud, jud, jud* of its rotor blades, thudding round.

'Hurry up, hurry up!' she fumed.

It could only be a matter of time before Avenger caught her up. But she still couldn't see it on the fire escape.

Any minute now the 'copter would be dropping a package to her. Inside there would be
seven tiny gravel-sized bits of stone. Each had
been chipped from a larger stone. These seven
larger stones were stored in one of RAAAA's
most secret vaults. But before that they had
been in the belly of a giant female crocodile.

All crocodiles have stones in their bellies
to help them grind up their food. But this
particular croc had been a legendary beast of
enormous strength and cunning. There were
many old stories about her.

The stories said she was so big and strong
that she could snatch an elephant from the
river bank. And so swift that the rest of
the elephant herd would only see the ripples
on the water. After the crocodile died someone slit it open and stole the seven stones.
The stones stayed hidden for a hundred
years until RAAAA discovered them, buried in
a secret cave.

The stories said also that whoever
swallowed the stones would gain the powers

of that formidable creature. No one knew for certain if that was true. No inspector had ever used them before. But none of them had ever faced anything as deadly as Avenger.

I hope those old stories aren't a load of codswallop, thought Mizz Z.

The 'copter's searchlights lit up Mizz Z on the museum roof. It swooped down, almost blinding her with its glare. The racket of the rotors was deafening, the wind from them like a mini-hurricane. Her clothes whipping around her, she crouched, shielding her one good eye.

And then the searchlights snapped off and the 'copter was gone, whirling away among the stars. Its *jud, jud, jud* was swallowed up by the constant hum of city traffic. Cautiously Mizz Z stood up and looked around.

'There it is!'

She'd known RAAAA wouldn't let her down. On the other side of the roof, beyond the cluster of old chimneys, was the small package, wrapped in bright yellow plastic.

Mizz Z hurried towards it . . .

Avenger was now squatting on the Friendship Arch, among the mythological monsters and dragons. When the big, noisy bird swooped off into the night, it saw its chance. Moving with incredible speed, it leaped onto the roof of the Money Tree bakery. The museum roof was still two storeys above it but Avenger didn't hesitate. It balanced along the roof ridge like a high-wire walker, then hurled itself at the wall of the much taller building next to the bakery. It began scuttling up like a giant spider, jabbing its spikes between the rough stones to help it hold on. When it got to the top, there would be one more mighty leap to make.

When Avenger came flying in out of the night, Mizz Z was ripping the wrapping off the package. She'd got down to a small brown envelope. Inside this she could see the tiny stones that might give her the strength to defeat the Crocodile King.

Mizz Z had spent years battling rogue

artefacts whose ancient powers had been regained. But this was the first time she'd tried to use some of these ancient powers for herself. She opened the envelope and peered inside. Her hands were shaking as she tipped the stones onto her palm.

There were seven pieces. They shone like tiny crystals.

Mizz Z swallowed hard. 'Careful, A. J. Zauyamakanda,' she warned herself. She didn't want to drop any of these precious stones. 'They look so pretty,' she marvelled.

No one could guess at the awesome power they contained.

Will this be enough? she wondered. RAAAA had only sent her a few fragments. And they had told her they were afraid that even this small dose would be more than the human body could stand. No one knew the effect they'd have on the person who took them.

But Mizz Z had no choice. It was her plan to defeat the Crocodile King and then take control of Avenger, just as Dr Cramp had tried to do. Dr Cramp had failed. And Mizz Z knew that even she, with her mighty talents, would fail too without the extra strength the stones could give her.

They'd better work! she thought desperately. It would mean the difference between life and death for her, Kapito, and the rest of her family.

Mizz Z thought of her niece, Betsy Zauyamakanda, who'd been such a tiny, wriggly baby that her family nickname was Bululu, or tadpole. Betsy had grown up to be a big strong girl and a dazzling football player, winning herself a trial for the ladies' national team. All the family were very proud.

But Betsy's hard work will count for nothing, she said to herself, *if I do not end this curse.*

At this moment, Betsy was thousands of miles away in Central Africa. But she would never be safe. She would spend her whole life looking over her shoulder. In the end, Avenger would find her, whichever country she was in. Borders, even oceans, were no barriers to the deadly tracker. It would find a way to cross them. Now it had been activated, it would never stop until its mission had been completed.

Mizz Z didn't hesitate any longer. She tipped the seven glittering crystals into her mouth and gulped them down.

There was a soft thud behind her on the museum roof. Her head whipped round. She caught a single flash of that metal Mohawk, then Avenger's net spun, frisbee-like, through the air. As it flew it seemed to expand into a great shimmering cloud. It dropped with deadly accuracy over her head and body.

Mizz Z was instantly trapped in its meshes, so tightly she couldn't move. She struggled violently, tried to rip the net with her fingers. But it wouldn't tear – it seemed as strong as steel cable.

And the more she struggled, the more she became entangled. She thought: *It's strangling me!* That dose of Crocodile Stones didn't seem to be making the slightest difference. She was as powerless before Avenger as a day-old kitten, and she was furious with herself. How had she let Avenger sneak up on her?

'You let it get too personal!' she raved at herself. 'You let your emotions take over!' Any Chief Inspector who did that always made mistakes.

Mizz Z stopped struggling and stood, sobbing for breath, swathed in net like an Egyptian mummy in bandages. Her one eye peeped through the mesh, blazing with helpless rage.

'Ancient artefact, my foot!' she screamed at Avenger. 'You're just a heap of scrapyard junk!'

Avenger's battered face didn't move. Only its blank eyes glowed brighter as it slid the bone whistle out of its ear lobe.

On the museum roof there was suddenly a deep, sinister hush. The wind dropped. The whole city seemed to go quiet, as if it were

191

waiting for something. Avenger put the whistle to its wooden lips, permanently fixed in that pointy-toothed snarl.

Every good tracker needs a dog, and now Avenger was summoning its own faithful hound. The name of this hound was *Darkness*. And its arrival always meant certain death for Avenger's victims.

Thin, eerie notes came from the bone whistle. That unearthly sound wasn't like human music. It seemed to reach out into the universe, calling to something from way beyond this world and time. Despite herself, Mizz Z felt her flesh creep and the hairs on the back of her neck lift. She watched, horrified, fascinated. How was Avenger blowing? Surely that couldn't be breath?

Then Mizz Z saw Avenger lift its glowing gaze to the heavens, as if expecting to see something up there. She slid her eye upwards too. She saw the pale silver moon suddenly turn a deep blood-red, like the end of the world was coming.

Down at ground level, Jin, Frankie and Mr Sparks were racing through the alleyways towards the museum.

Jin had heard the helicopter swoop by. But he hadn't given it a second thought. He hadn't even looked up. There were often police 'copters about, especially at night, buzzing over the city.

Jin would have noticed, though, if the moon had become blood-red. So would Frankie and Dad. But it didn't. To them it looked just the same as before: pale and silver and cold. But Jin's sharp eyes did spot something, chucked away between the wheelie bins. He pounced on it.

'It's Mizz Z's flip-flop,' he said, holding it up. 'And here's the other one.'

'You don't think that means Avenger's got her?' Frankie's voice was small and shaky.

'No,' Dad reassured her. 'She probably just ditched them so she could run faster.'

Frankie snatched them from Jin: 'I'll carry those.'

They weren't just ordinary flip-flops. Mizz Z had told Frankie on their last adventure that they were made from the tyres of a wrecked army jeep. That was after she'd complimented Frankie on her customized clothes. 'Girl, I like your style. It is spot on!' she had told her. Frankie would never forget those words. Coming from Mizz Z, who never praised unless she meant it, they were worth more than gold.

'I'll give these back to her when we find her,' Frankie announced confidently to Jin.

She didn't speak the rest of her thoughts, which were: *If we find her alive, if Avenger didn't get her already*.

Up on the museum roof, Mizz Z gazed at the blood-red moon above her.

'What on earth's happening?' she whispered in an awe-stricken voice.

Feelings of dread had now replaced her rage, clutching her mind with icy fingers. She tried to fight her fear, like she usually did. But this time, it wouldn't go away.

From the west, a sinister black storm cloud appeared. There was no wind at all; it shouldn't be moving. But it was. Like some ghostly ship, it sailed across the sky. As it passed, the sparkling stars were extinguished. The moon, a fiery red ball, still hung above the museum. But the cloud stopped over that and eclipsed it too. For a moment, the world was plunged into darkness. It was pitch-black on the roof.

Only Avenger's eyes pierced the dark, their twin yellow beams slanting upwards like searchlights.

Mizz Z, wrapped in her net shroud, felt her blood freezing in her veins. She knew that whatever was coming was much, much stronger than her. That it was some kind of elemental force with more than human, more than earthly powers that could squash her like an insect. She tried to face it defiantly, with that proud tilt of her chin.

'Have courage!' she ordered herself. 'Remember you are a Chief Inspector!'

From right overhead came a deep, rumbling growl as if a thunderstorm was about to break. The cloud that hid the red moon was changing shape. Now a dark beast's head, more wolf than dog, appeared in the night sky. Light streamed through its eye holes from the moon behind, as if they were pouring rivers of burning blood.

'Darkness!' murmured Mizz Z, aghast, at last understanding the words of that dying man in the ancient stories.

Darkness opened its jaws like a fiery pit leaping with flames. It seemed it could gobble up planets, galaxies. But Mizz Z knew it had come only for her, to fulfil the Croc King's curse.

Then the growl came again, echoing across the heavens. It was so menacing, so spine-chilling that it seemed to Mizz Z like the sound of doom.

And then the panic really kicked in. Darkness came hurtling down like a comet, trailing flames, getting bigger the closer to Earth it came. Its great jaws gaped wider to swallow Mizz Z in one gulp.

She felt her heart stopping, her body shutting down from the shock. It seemed that Mizz Z would die of terror, like all Avenger's victims. She went limp and slumped in her net bindings, falling to her knees. Her life flashed before her. She saw her village when she was a girl, smelled wood smoke, fried bananas and roasting groundnuts. Then there was only Darkness . . .

But, in a split second, everything changed.

Mizz Z felt her heart suddenly jerk back to life and begin beating strongly. Warm blood was pulsing again in her veins! Amazing new powers surged through her mind and body. The Crocodile Stones were working, just when she'd given up hope.

Mizz Z ripped the net. The mesh parted like candyfloss and fell around her. Free at last, she sprang from her prison and stood tall on the roof. She pointed an accusing finger and screamed into the sky in Chewa, 'Dark-ness, be gone!'

Darkness stopped dead in its blazing descent. It hung suspended just above the roof, filling the city sky.

But now Mizz Z had her own ancient powers to help her fight this dreadful curse. The spirit of that legendary lady croc burned in her body. She felt strong and cunning. Her natural courage and confidence had increased ten thousand times. She felt invincible, scared of nothing, man or beast or ghost. Mizz Z was back in control.

She commanded Darkness again with a disdainful wave of her hand, 'Be gone! Bad dog!'

Immediately the fiery lights went out. Instead of flames, Darkness had huge gaping holes for its eyes and mouth. Through them you could see the navy-blue sky with stars twinkling again. The moon changed back from blood-red to palest silver. The dog head hung there for a few seconds like a huge black mask.

Then it whisked off backwards into the heavens, getting further and further away from Earth until it was lost among the stars.

'Good riddance,' said Mizz Z, rubbing her hands.

Did she hear Darkness whimpering as it went? For the rest of her life she was never sure about that. But she could hear the sounds of the city again: the traffic hum below her, the rattle of passing trains. As if it was just an ordinary night.

Then Avenger, Darkness's master, sprang out of the shadows, metal glinting all over its squat wooden body. Its gleaming eyes gazed after Darkness, as if it couldn't believe what had happened. Then it turned them again on its quarry.

'Hello, Avenger,' said Mizz Z coolly, deliberately backing away towards the edge of the roof.

Now she had to deal with the fearsome tracker. It would never give up. She knew she might not escape for a second time. When it netted her again and then whistled for Darkness she might have lost the powers the Crocodile Stones had given her. She had no idea how long those powers would last. Minutes? An hour? A day? RAAAA had warned her that even they didn't know. And the old stories didn't say.

'Get a move on, A. J. Zauyamakanda,' Mizz Z ordered herself as she stared into Avenger's eyes. She *must* defeat the Crocodile King before her extra powers ran out. 'And then it will be your turn,' she told Avenger in English. 'Because, when I have defeated the king, I will claim his possessions. You will belong to me. And you will have to do what I say.'

But for the next few minutes, at least, she wanted the deadly tracker out of the way.

Avenger stalked her, in its panther crouch, as she walked very slowly backwards, even closer to the roof edge. On the way, its spiky hand picked up its tattered net, which, to Mizz Z's astonishment, seemed to mend itself as she watched – it was a perfect circle again. Avenger had its bone whistle in its other hand, ready.

'Oh no, you don't!' snarled Mizz Z, baring her teeth, just like Avenger's.

That legendary lady croc could easily snatch a lion from the river bank. With the same speed and ferocity, Mizz Z leaped at Avenger, grabbed the bone whistle out of its hand and hurled it away. It went whirling through space, then fell down into the dark streets below.

Avenger's face was immobile, as always. But its yellow disc eyes lingered on Mizz Z for about two seconds. Was there some expression in them? Did they look surprised, even impressed, at her resistance?

Of course not, thought Mizz Z. *Avenger doesn't have feelings. It's just a mechanical thing. A machine.*

Then it leaped over the roof edge and into the night, to get its whistle back.

Mizz Z had no time to look down to see

where Avenger had gone. She rushed to the fire door. But it was closed again and there was no way to open it from the outside.

'That is rather inconvenient,' she said, clicking her tongue in annoyance. Then she remembered her new super-strength and kicked in the fire door. *Bam! Bam! Bam!* Her bare feet shattered it to matchsticks. '*Hmmm.*' Mizz Z raised one eyebrow slightly. 'These Crocodile Stones are quite effective.'

She picked her way through the piles of splintered wood. No sirens had shrilled through the building when she destroyed the door. The police had thought the alarm system was faulty, so hadn't re-set it before they left.

Good, thought Mizz Z. She didn't want the police turning up again, crawling all over the building. That might complicate matters. 'It will be just the two of us. Crocodile Queen versus Crocodile King,' she declared grimly as she padded downstairs, heading for that small room off the main hall and the ancient baobab tree.

Outside the museum, Avenger had found its whistle again. It slotted it back into its ear. It would need to call Darkness again, very soon. It raised its battered face and seemed to sniff the air. It couldn't sense Mizz Z's fear any more, couldn't track her down by her terror. So it bent its metal-crested head and sniffed at the pink and orange rag tied to the nail in its chest, reminding itself of Mizz Z's scented hair oil. Then it lifted its head again. Very faintly it could smell frangipani on the air. Its prey was somewhere close.

Its roughly hacked features showed no expression. Only its glowing eyes flashed once, twice.

With a clink of metal, it dropped into its panther crouch and prowled around the building, looking for a quick way in.

Chapter Thirteen

As Mizz Z headed for the Crocodile King's lair, Jin and Frankie were hurrying across the City Museum car park. Their clothes were cold and soggy, their shoes squelched water at every step. Neither of them noticed.

Frankie clutched Mizz Z's flip-flops to her as she ran, as if she was carrying something precious.

'Where's Dad?' asked Jin.

Frankie took one glance behind. 'He'll catch up,' she said. 'Come on, we can't wait.'

Jin raced round the side of the museum. But the door marked PRIVATE wouldn't open – the police had locked it again before they left. Jin hammered on it frantically and yelled, 'Mizz Z! Doctor Cramp! Are you in there?'

No one answered. 'What do we do now?' he asked.

Then from the other side of the building came the crash of breaking glass. Jin and Frankie shot an alarmed look at each other before starting to run towards the sound.

Jin was lurching about a lot now. His legs seemed to go in all directions. 'Come on, come on!' he urged himself, angry and frustrated. Why did this always happen when he got tired?

He caught Frankie up round the corner. She was staring at a big ground-floor window. It had exploded. Broken glass was scattered everywhere, gleaming in the moonlight. Only a few jagged bits were left in the frame.

'Think Mizz Z did this?' she asked Jin.

Jin forgot about his slow running. Tracking took over his mind. Calmly he inspected the damage, searching for clues. And when he spoke, his voice rang with confidence. Suddenly, in all the craziness going on around him, he knew something for *certain*. There were rusty scrapes on the stone window ledge, greasy marks on the wall, and Jin spotted something snagged on a glass splinter – a few wispy fibres from the rotting rags tied onto Avenger's spikes. 'No,' he told Frankie. 'It was Avenger. It punched a hole though the window and climbed in.'

'You *sure* it was Avenger?' Frankie challenged him. 'You sure it was climbing in, not out?' Those terrors were invading her mind again. If it was climbing out, maybe it had already done its job and terminated Mizz Z.

Jin pointed to the flower border below the window. 'See its footprints? They only lead up to the window. There's none leading away.'

Frankie stared at Jin, impressed. 'You're right, bro'. That's really clever.'

'Naa, it's easy,' said Jin, shrugging modestly. 'You just have to look for signs.'

'If Avenger's gone in there,' said Frankie, chewing away at her nails, 'that means Mizz Z's already inside.'

'And she must still be alive,' Jin agreed.

Hope flickered again in Frankie's eyes: 'We've got to find her before it does.'

'Maybe we should wait for Dad,' said Jin. 'I can see him coming.'

But, with Mizz Z's flip-flops dangling from her hand, Frankie was already climbing through the broken window. By the time Jin and Dad caught up with her, she was rushing through the 'Toilets of the World' exhibition.

Moonbeams spilled through the tall windows, filling the hall with grotesque shadows that twisted and writhed over the walls and across the ceiling.

'Wait!' Dad puffed. He put a hand on Frankie's shoulder. 'Where's that Avenger thing? Have you seen it?'

Frankie shook her head and wriggled away. She had eyes only for Mizz Z. She could see her in the small room, lit up by silver moonlight, standing tall and majestic next to the baobab. The Chief Inspector held the crocodile mask in her hands. Its long, dangling palm fronds trailed on the floor.

'Mizz Z!' yelled Frankie.

Mizz Z turned and saw them. She didn't seem surprised they were here, but she commanded, 'Don't come near! You cannot help me. I alone must run the risks.'

Frankie skidded to a halt. When Mizz Z spoke in that imperious voice, with her face so forbidding, you had better obey.

Jin stopped too. He started shaking – he couldn't help it. It was the same menace he'd felt before. But this time it was much, much stronger. It seemed to come surging out of the small room like a toxic tide.

'Want your shoes?' Frankie asked Mizz Z in a very small voice, holding up the flip-flops.

But Mizz Z didn't seem to hear. Her amber eye was already sliding aside, as if she were in another world, far away from them, where they couldn't follow and trivial details like shoes didn't concern her. She lifted the mask with both arms and dropped it over her head. Now her face was that of a crocodile, her body hidden by the palm fronds. From deep inside the wooden jaws a single eye glittered.

Then nothing happened. Mizz Z seemed to be waiting.

'What's she doing?' hissed Dad.

'Taking on the Crocodile King,' Frankie told him in a tense whisper, without taking her eyes off Mizz Z. 'It's the only way to end the curse on her family.'

'This is madness,' hissed Dad. 'I'm going to put a stop to it.'

'No,' begged Frankie. 'Stay out of it, Dad. Mizz Z knows what she's doing.'

'But he'll take her over,' said Jin. 'Like he did to Doctor Cramp.'

A sudden banging and crashing of porcelain and stainless steel came from inside the baobab. It was much louder than before, as if the Croc King's spirit was getting very worked up and excited.

'That's him!' said Jin. 'He's coming!'

The door in the trunk burst open. Jin's sharp eyes spotted the rippling air as the Crocodile King left the baobab, and he hurled himself forward with some kind of crazy idea of blocking the king's path to Mizz Z.

But the king's spirit just flowed round him. The ancient ruler was ravenously hungry for power. And this time, when he invaded the mind and body of the mask-wearer, nothing was going to drive him out.

From inside the crocodile mask Mizz Z was wearing came a howl of triumph, then a furious torrent of Chewa. Jin and Frankie threw a horrified glance at each other.

'He's done it,' whispered Jin in an anguished voice. 'I told you.'

The king was too powerful, it seemed, even for the mighty Mizz Z. It was as if he'd instantly gobbled up her mind and claimed her body as his own.

'Wait,' Frankie remembered. 'She's got something to help her. Crocodile Stones from RAAAA.'

'What use are they?' Jin demanded.

'I don't know,' Frankie admitted. 'I don't know.'

They could only watch as the Crocodile King whirled Mizz Z's body around in a manic dance. He was screaming with triumph at being flesh and blood again, spitting with fury at being shut up for so long in his baobab prison.

Frankie's nerve broke at last. 'We've got to help her!' She was already sprinting towards the small room when suddenly there was a glint of metal. Avenger sprang from a shadowy corner and landed right in front of Frankie. Its glowing eyes were fixed on her and its wooden fingers clasped its net, which was now slowly unfurling.

'Get back!' Dad and Jin yelled at Frankie.

Carefully, not making any sudden moves, Frankie stepped backwards, every second expecting Avenger to throw its net. But it didn't. It just stood blocking their way to the small room. They could see everything that was going on. But they couldn't do a single thing to help.

Mizz Z, thought Jin in despair. Would she

ever come back? Or was she gone for ever? He just couldn't believe it. That the fabulous Mizz Z, who'd exploded into his life like a firework display, could get snuffed out so quickly, like a sputtering candle.

Then Dad said, 'Look!'

Jin stared. He screwed his fists around in his eyes, convinced they were playing tricks. Then stared again.

Frankie didn't believe it, either. 'What's happening?' she stammered, bewildered.

Because the figure in front of them seemed to be transforming. The tatty palm fronds changed to olive-green, scaly skin. The shabby wooden mask became a great armoured head with savage teeth. From nowhere a long, thrashing tail appeared. Suddenly a monster croc, rearing up on its hind legs, seemed to fill the room.

'Is it real?' breathed Frankie. Or was it just an illusion? Nothing was as it seemed when ancient powers were released.

Jin took two steps towards the small room.

'Stay back!' warned Dad. The huge croc was growling like a dog and whipping the air wildly with its tail. Avenger, standing on guard, was letting more of its net unfold. All they could do was stay at a safe distance and watch.

Things happened then with horrifying swiftness. Jin's head was spinning, his brain just couldn't keep up. Now the monster croc was a wooden mask again, with the Croc King roaring out in Chewa, then it swapped back again to the scaly, olive-green reptile, then wooden mask, then monster croc in a dizzying switchover, while the room echoed with ferocious growls and spine-chilling Chewa curses.

'Mizz Z's fighting back!' yelled Frankie.

Then the monster croc seemed to come out on top. It dropped down on all fours and slithered out into the main hall. Avenger stood aside to let it pass.

'Stay back!' yelled Dad again.

But the great beast wasn't after them. It

appeared to be battling some invisible enemy of its own, twisting over on the tiles, smashing the exhibits to bits, its tail thrashing in the death rolls that crocs do to tear their prey apart, its great jaws snapping at something they couldn't see.

It stopped death-rolling, raised itself up on its scaly feet and ran, its great armour-plated head crashing like a battering ram through the swing door. Then it was gone, slithering down the steps that led to the museum cellar.

Now Avenger was on the move too!

'Watch out!' yelled Jin.

But like the great croc the deadly tracker didn't even give them a glance. It went springing to the door with its wolf-like lope and followed the crocodile down to the cellar.

For a minute, Jin, Dad and Frankie stood in the wreckage of toilets, just staring at each other, too stunned to speak.

It was Frankie who recovered first. 'I'm going after it,' she said, and vanished through the door.

'Wait, Frankie!' said Jin. But his sister's biker boots were already thudding down the stairs.

Jin and Dad caught up with her down in the museum cellar. She was standing among the packing cases, her face lit up in the dim yellow light. She was staring, aghast, at a big jagged hole in the wall where the grille had been. There were bricks scattered all around.

'It's smashed through into the bakery,' she said.

'Careful,' said Dad as they crept through too. 'It might be just on the other side.'

In the bakery cellar, there was evidence everywhere of an epic battle. Sacks of bun-making stuff were burst and shredded. Metal bun-steaming trays were crushed like Coke cans, as if they'd been chomped between bone-crushing jaws.

Jin coughed, straining to see through the choking white clouds of flour. 'I don't think it's here,' he said as the flour began to settle. There was no sign of Avenger, either.

Then they heard more crashing, very close by.

'It's in the kitchen!' said Frankie, running.

'I'll go first,' said Dad. But the headstrong Frankie was already inside.

When Jin and Dad joined her, she was standing, staring. There was silence in the bakery kitchen, like the hush after a terrific storm. It was only broken by the hissing of the great Iron Dragon that loomed above them all, king of the kitchen.

Woks and other kitchen implements were strewn all over the place. The monster croc was nowhere to be seen. But in the middle of all the destruction stood a single figure – the mask-wearer, in the shabby wooden crocodile head and palm-frond cape.

It was Mizz Z's body – there was no doubt of that, you could see her bare feet and arms, with her glittering bronze bracelets. But was the Crocodile King still in control of her?

Jin watched, hardly daring to breathe, waiting for the king's deep, angry voice to come from the mask's wooden jaws. His hands were clenched into fists with the strain, his fingernails stabbing his palms until they bled.

'Who won?' he asked Frankie in a frantic whisper.

'I don't know. Wait, something's happening.'

Slowly the mask-wearer lifted off the wooden head. Mizz Z's face was revealed.

'Speak to us, Mizz Z,' begged Jin.

Mizz Z drew herself up to her full height. Her chin tilted in that proud, defiant way they knew so well. 'With the help of the Crocodile Stones,' she told them, 'I have fought the Crocodile King and won!'

'Yay!' yelled Jin, leaping up and wildly punching the air.

Could it be tears of joy Frankie was dashing away from her eyes? You could be sure she would never admit it.

'Hey, Mizz Z,' she said, in her coolest, most off-hand manner, 'want your flip-flops back now?'

Jin was so busy celebrating that even he

didn't spot the ripples in the air as the defeated Croc King's spirit fled the scene, slipping through the ventilation grille in the kitchen ceiling to the street outside.

The Crocodile King had been driven out of the mask-wearer. But he had come too far from the baobab to survive – he would shrivel to nothing before he got back there. Then, amazingly, he found a home in another ancient tree. It was just a metre away, proudly displayed in a blue and white pot beside the bakery door.

It wasn't as grand or spacious as the baobab; it was hardly what the Crocodile King was used to. But it was either that or total oblivion. So the king's spirit reluctantly took refuge inside the Tangs' lucky money tree.

Down in the kitchen of the bakery Dad was staring around at the wreckage. 'What on earth,' he was wondering, 'are Auntie and Uncle going to say when they see all this?'

Chapter Fourteen

Dad quickly forgot about what Auntie and Uncle would think, because Jin said, 'Watch out!'

He'd heard a sound from a corner. It was the rasping of metal.

'Avenger,' he warned.

First they saw the sheen of its smooth oiled skull, the flash of that warlike metal crest. Then Avenger itself leaped out of the shadows, its robot eyes on full beam, its bone teeth fixed in that sinister snarl.

Its eyes locked on Mizz Z with an unblinking stare.

Jin felt sick with despair and horror. *It's still out to get her*, he thought. *Would that wooden freak never, ever give up?*

'Didn't you end the curse,' whispered Frankie in a shaky voice, 'when you defeated the Crocodile King?'

'Not quite,' Mizz Z answered. 'I need to deal with Avenger now.'

But she'd better do it fast. The Crocodile Stones had given her a big blast of extra strength. For a short time she was like a super-woman – she could have taken on the world, the universe! But she could feel that power already draining away. *RAAAA should have sent me a bigger dose*, she thought.

Avenger was level with Jin now. They were exactly the same height.

'Don't move, son,' warned Dad. 'Don't get in its way.'

But Jin just couldn't help it; he let his eyes slide over to the statue. Suddenly it didn't look ancient at all. It looked like a seriously cool, modern work of art, recycled from scrapyard materials. But that crazy thought went straight out of Jin's head when he remembered that this thing was trying to kill Mizz Z.

'Run!' Jin hissed frantically at Mizz Z. 'Why don't you run?'

'No,' said Mizz Z firmly. 'As I told Frankie before, I will not run all my life.' She met Avenger's gaze without flinching, her head held high. But all the time Jin could see that nerve fluttering in her cheek, just under the eye which she'd lost to Zilombo, that other ancient monster.

Jin's nerves were doing more than flutter. They seemed to be shrieking out loud as he waited for Avenger to throw its net.

But it didn't. It didn't even drop into its panther crouch. Instead, with surprising gracefulness, it bent at the waist and lowered its crested head, its spiky arms spread wide, palms upward.

Behind Mizz Z, the mighty Iron Dragon was waking early from its night-time snooze. Flames whooshed up in the furnace like a blowtorch. As their heat spread through its body the Iron Dragon seemed to come alive. Smoke snorted from its nostrils, fire dancing behind its fierce, goggly eyes.

But Jin didn't notice. He was too busy watching Avenger. He couldn't believe what he saw.

'It's bowing to you!' he said, amazed.

Mizz Z acknowledged Avenger's bow with a dignified nod of her head.

Frankie stared, mystified. Just a minute ago the Croc King's personal assassin had been Mizz Z's deadly enemy, on a mission to hunt her down. Now it stood quietly before her. The glow in its eyes faded from golden to yellow.

'What's happening?' hissed Frankie.

'Avenger is waiting for new instructions,' said Mizz Z. 'A bit like a computer on standby.' She gave a long, secret sigh of relief. She'd never been one hundred per cent sure that, when she'd defeated the Crocodile King, Avenger would bow before her and acknowledge her as its master. You never knew with these ancient artefacts. They could be really awkward customers.

'Waiting for whose instructions?' asked Jin.

'Mine,' said Mizz Z, with more than a hint of pride in her voice. 'I have defeated its master, the Crocodile King, so now I must tell it what to do.'

Frankie said, 'Then tell it to leave you and your family alone.'

Mizz Z replied, 'It is rather more complicated than that. Avenger only works in certain ways. One must observe the ancient rituals.' Then she commanded, 'Get me a sharp piece of metal.'

'I'll get it,' said Jin, dashing past Dad and the Iron Dragon. He rummaged in the cutlery drawer. *Sharp*, he thought, *it's got to be sharp*.

There were all kinds of sharp things in there, including huge, scary chopping knives. But when Jin hurtled back to Mizz Z he found his fingers had somehow missed the chopping knives and he was grasping a metal spoon for draining noodles instead.

But Mizz Z said, as she took it from him, 'That will be perfect.' With the last of the strength from that legendary lady croc's stones, she snapped the noodle spoon in half to make a sharp edge.

Suddenly, as Frankie gazed, still baffled, a light seemed to click on in her brain. 'Bet I know what you're going to do now,' she told Mizz Z triumphantly. 'You're giving Avenger a new mission.'

Mizz Z took the time to flash an approving glance in her direction. 'Spot on,' she told Frankie. 'I must replace the Zauyamakanda curse with one of my own. I must give it a new enemy to hunt down.'

'But who are you going to curse?' asked Frankie.

'I don't know,' said Mizz Z. 'It is rather a problem.'

'What about that creepy Doctor Cramp?' said Jin. 'All this is his fault. He brought the Croc King's spirit to this country.'

'I could give you a whole list of people who need cursing. There's—' began Frankie.

'No,' Dad interrupted. 'That's right out of order.'

'Your father is quite correct,' said Mizz Z. 'It cannot be a living person.' Despite herself, she shuddered as she remembered Darkness. 'Anyone I cursed would almost certainly end up dead. I cannot be responsible for that.'

Jin wrinkled his face in concentration.

Behind him the Iron Dragon was rumbling, clanking and spitting fire and steam, like some ancient mechanical monster. And it was then that Jin had his brilliant idea. He was so full of dread and excitement that he could barely blurt it out.

'Curse the Iron Dragon!' he told Mizz Z. 'Avenger versus Iron Dragon, see? Two machines against each other. Nobody gets hurt.'

'What are you talking about?' said Frankie.

But Mizz Z threw a startled look at Jin. She seemed to be struggling in her own mind. Chief Inspectors should protect ancient artefacts – not set them against each other.

225

You've got no choice, she told herself. She had to find Avenger another target, and quickly. 'That is a truly inspired idea,' she told Jin. 'Fire up the dragon!' she cried. 'Put more coal into the furnace.'

Jin hurled himself forward in his usual headlong rush when Dad pushed him gently aside. 'It's OK, son. I'll do it.' He strode to the pile of coal next to the bun-steaming stove and grabbed a shovel. He used it to prise open the furnace door. Heat came blasting out, almost frying his eyeballs. The glow from the blazing coals stained his face ghastly red as he began stoking the furnace.

Meanwhile, Mizz Z had picked up the mask from the floor where she'd laid it. She stroked its withered palm fronds.

'Wait a minute.' Frankie shuddered. 'You don't have to put that on again, do you?'

Mizz Z nodded. 'I'm afraid I must. It's part of the ritual. Without it, I can't send Avenger on its new mission.'

'But how do you know the king's spirit has

really gone?' Jin demanded. 'What if it's still hanging around somewhere?'

'The king is gone for good,' said Mizz Z. 'As I told you, without a home his spirit will shrivel away.' Her voice sounded super-confident. Even though a little voice whispered, inside her head, 'Are you *sure* he's gone?'

With a king as cunning and power mad as him, who could ever be certain?

Jin, too, was seriously worried. 'But what if he tries to take you over again?'

'Then she'll just fight him off,' Frankie told Jin, 'like she did before. Won't you, Mizz Z?'

Mizz Z didn't answer. Now wasn't the time to tell them that if the king did launch another attack, try to invade her mind, she wouldn't be able to defend herself. The power the Crocodile Stones had given her was gone completely. *Just be quick, A. J. Zauyamakanda,* she urged herself, dropping the crocodile mask over her head.

As Avenger stood, unmoving, Mizz Z pulled out the silver nail the Crocodile King had hammered in. She pushed the spoon handle into the statue's wooden chest. The handle gleamed, shiny and polished, among the other rusty bits of metal, grisly reminders of all the people that Avenger had netted and Darkness had scared to death.

In the old money tree on the pavement, just metres above Mizz Z, the Croc King's spirit was getting excited.

Mizz Z squatted, until the mask was level with Avenger's battered face. She began whispering to the tracker in old Chewa, in a low chanting voice, just as the Crocodile King had done.

Outside the bakery door, the money tree was shaking. Any second now the air would ripple as the Crocodile King slipped out and back down through the grille to the kitchen. He sensed that Mizz Z was much weaker than before. He knew this time he would win . . .

But there came footsteps. Mr Lu, from the Lotus Flower, gazed anxiously around. The street was in darkness. It was 3.30 a.m. All the restaurants and shops were closed up. There was no one to see him taking the lucky money tree to his own bakery. 'I'm only *borrowing* it,' he excused himself. '*Ugh!*' he grunted as he stooped to pick up the heavy blue and white pot the Tangs' money tree was planted in. 'This is breaking my back!'

As he staggered along, Mr Lu had no idea that he'd just thwarted the Croc King's latest plans to become flesh and blood. The king couldn't leave the tree now – he was too far away from the mask-wearer. He would shrivel up trying to get there. So he was trapped, once again, inside an ancient tree – only this one was Chinese instead of African. Once again, he'd failed to win back his former power. And he was absolutely raging mad about that.

'That'll show those toffee-nosed Tangs!' crowed Mr Lu as he hid the money tree in a back room. 'Now they'll lose all their luck and the Lotus Flower will be the most successful bakery in Chinatown.'

But already the furious Crocodile King was sending out bad vibes, flesh-crawling feelings of menace and fear that soon filled the small room and began to spread out through the rest of the bakery.

Next morning, to Mr Lu's dismay, business at the Lotus Flower would be worse than ever. All his customers fled, shaking and ashen-faced, crying, 'I felt really afraid. I just had to get out of there!'

Chapter Fifteen

Back in the Tangs' bakery, Mizz Z's ritual was complete. Avenger's eyes suddenly clicked on full beam, glowing again like two golden coins.

Mizz Z sighed with relief. It seemed like the new curse had finally worked. And the Crocodile King hadn't attempted a takeover. Thankfully she took off the crocodile mask.

Avenger's head swivelled round, its net already unfolding.

'Mr Sparks,' commanded Mizz Z. 'Move away from the Iron Dragon.'

Dad, sweat dripping from his face, stepped backwards. The Iron Dragon was way, way beyond bun-steaming temperature. Its furnace was glowing white-hot. No one had ever fired it up to these dangerous levels. It looked like a volcano about to blow.

Avenger dropped into its hunting crouch.

'Stay exactly where you are,' Mizz Z warned Jin, Frankie and their dad. 'Whatever you do, don't get in its way.'

Frankie stared at the Iron Dragon clanking and roaring above them. Since way before she was born, it had ruled the Money Tree bakery and had Uncle and Auntie scurrying around, waiting on it like slaves.

Everyone thought it was indestructible. That Uncle would never get rid of it. That it would be here for ever, driving Auntie to despair with its sulks and tantrums, demanding attention all the time.

'What's going to happen?' Frankie asked Mizz Z.

'Avenger will try to destroy the Iron Dragon,' said Mizz Z.

'We should get out of here now,' said Dad. 'This is going to get nasty.'

'Wait,' warned Mizz Z, 'until Avenger has made its move.'

Avenger slowly turned its wooden head. The bear grease was wearing off now and its joints were starting to get stiff and creaky again.

Jin found himself staring straight into the deadly tracker's face. He almost gasped out loud. Because he saw something – some expression, a flicker just for a second in those ancient eyes that had always been blank before.

Shocked to the core, Jin thought, *That can't be right! You made a mistake*, he told himself. *Look again*. But he never got the chance because Avenger, with one great spring, leaped into the Iron's Dragon's furnace. The heavy metal door swung shut behind it.

Jin, Frankie and Dad gazed, mesmerized.

Jin cried out, 'What's it doing? The Dragon will burn it up!'

'Good,' said Frankie.

But the Dragon wasn't finding it that easy. The noise was ear-splitting. It seemed as if a war was going on inside the belly of the great iron beast. It roared like a T. Rex under attack while its jaws spurted flames and steam. From inside the furnace came zinging sounds like machine-gun bullets while the ovens clanged like gongs, and black smoke billowed out into the kitchen.

Dad was yelling something but no one could hear what he was saying in all the din and chaos.

Jin was crouching, coughing and covering his head. Then the Dragon's snaky body started to rock. Jin hung giddily onto a kitchen unit. The cellar floor was heaving, the flag-stones cracking as if an earthquake had started. The tip of an iron tail snapped off and flew over Jin's head like a red-hot spear to stick, quivering, in the wall.

'Move!' yelled Mizz Z. 'The Dragon is breaking up!' And she led the way, slap-slapping in her flip-flops up the steps into the bakery. She was going to smash the glass front door so they could escape. But Frankie, rummaging in her pockets, said, 'I've got a key,' and she let them out into the cool night air of Chinatown.

'Careful!' warned Dad as Jin squatted down to spy through the grille in the pavement.

Jin leaped back just in time. From underground, there came a dull booming sound. The ground shook and with a roaring *Whoosh!* a fountain of flames shot through the grille, then just as quickly died back. The echoes of the boom faded too. A shower of red sparks flew up and whisked away down the street. Then some thick, grey, creeping smoke. Then nothing, except a smell of burning and silence.

Along the street, some lights were being switched on in bedrooms.

Dad had already phoned the fire brigade. Now he was on his mobile, calling Auntie and Uncle Tang. 'I'll tell them there's been an accident,' he said.

'You're not going to tell them the truth, are you?' asked Jin. 'About the Crocodile King and Avenger?'

'If he tried to,' said Frankie, 'they'd never believe it. They'd think he'd gone crazy.' She scarcely believed it herself, even though she'd seen it all happen with her own eyes.

Mizz Z knelt down on the pavement to peer through the grille. 'It is over,' she said in a flat and expressionless voice.

'Has Avenger been destroyed?' asked Jin.

'Yes, it has finally claimed its last victim,' Mizz Z confirmed. 'Now we Zauyamakandas can sleep safely in our beds.'

Frankie gave a whoop of glee. 'Good riddance!' she said. 'Hey, well done, Mizz Z, bet you knew it would end up burned to cinders.'

'Yes, I thought that might happen,' Mizz Z admitted.

But Jin, with his skill at sensing people's moods, knew that Mizz Z didn't share Frankie's triumph. 'Are you sad?' he asked Mizz Z.

'Sad?' said Frankie. 'What a stupid question.'

But Mizz Z gave a heavy sigh. 'My little Jin,' she said. 'I can't hide anything from you, can I? I confess that I wish I hadn't had to destroy it. RAAAA will not be pleased. It's my job to protect ancient artefacts. And, of course, the mask has been burned to cinders. And that's not even counting the Iron Dragon.'

'You didn't have a choice,' said Frankie. 'Don't beat yourself up about it. And no one cares about the Dragon. It made Auntie's life a misery.'

But Mizz Z didn't hear her. She seemed haunted by what she'd had to do – it went against all the rules of RAAAA. And worse, she'd done it for personal rather than professional reasons.

'Come on, Mizz Z!' said Frankie, her voice growing shriller as she relived in her mind how she'd almost drowned when she'd fled from Avenger onto the mud flats. Her clothes were still damp. She still had river weed in her hair. 'You did the world a favour. That horrible freaky *thing*,' she spat out furiously. 'I mean, I don't even know *what* it was—'

Mizz Z interrupted, to stop Frankie getting more worked up. 'It was just a machine,' she said firmly, 'used by the Crocodile King to hunt down those he cursed. And now it is gone. No one needs to be scared of it any more.'

'*Just a machine*.' Jin murmured Mizz Z's words to himself. He recalled what he'd seen in Avenger's eyes just seconds before it had leaped into the furnace. Jin often blurted out his thoughts without thinking. But even he knew now wasn't the time to speak about that.

'Anyway, it *had* to be destroyed,' Frankie insisted. 'It's a no-brainer.'

'I wish,' said Mizz Z, in a very quiet voice they could hardly hear, 'that I was as sure about that as you.' Suddenly she seemed to be drooping with exhaustion, as if she didn't even have the strength left to haul herself to her feet.

'You all right, Mizz Z?' asked Frankie, forgetting her own terrors.

'Yes. I am just rather weary, that's all,' replied the Chief Inspector. 'It has been a long night.'

Frankie and Jin knelt beside her on the scorched pavement. Now the panic was over, now there was nothing, Mizz Z said, to fear, they felt shattered too. Jin could have curled up right there and gone to sleep.

Behind them they could hear Dad saying, 'Yes, I'm afraid the Iron Dragon seems to have blown itself up. No, no, only the kitchen was damaged. Lucky those old cellar walls are so thick. They seem to have contained the blast. Yes, yes, the fire engines are on their way. How did I discover the fire? I just happened to be doing an emergency call-out nearby.'

'Tell Mr and Mrs Tang,' Mizz Z roused herself to say, 'that the damage will all be paid for.'

Jin gazed down through the grille. The mighty Iron Dragon was in ruins – just a mangled mountain of smoking black metal. Here and there in the wreckage Jin could make out a great clawed foot, a bit of scaly tail and a bun-steaming shelf.

There was no sign of Avenger.

Had its wooden body really been burned to ashes? The deadly tracker had been so relentless, so unstoppable. *Maybe*, Jin was beginning to think, *it somehow survived*.

Then something rolled clinking out of the iron tangle. It was a couple of big metal spikes from Avenger's Mohawk, scorched black by the fire.

So it's really gone, thought Jin, relief flooding through his body.

But, like Mizz Z, a part of him felt sorry. Jin had learned something about himself tonight. He'd learned that he was good at tracking, at looking for signs – it had really amazed him. But Avenger had been better than good – it had been the best tracker in the world, ever.

'Respect,' he whispered to the remains of Avenger, down on the cellar floor.

Then Jin's sharp eyes spotted something. It was lying by the grille, practically nudging his hand, as if he was meant to find it. With a look of wonder on his face, he picked it up. It was black with soot, so he cleaned it on his T-shirt.

'Look,' he told Mizz Z, holding up the tiny yellow bone tube. 'It's the thing Avenger wore through its ear.' He looked at it closer, turning it over in his palm. 'Hey! It's got holes in it. It looks like a little whistle. Wonder what happens if—' And he held it up to his lips to blow.

'No!' cried Mizz Z in horror, snatching it from him.

Jin was amazed to see that the mighty Mizz Z was shaking. 'What is it?' he asked, dismayed. 'What's wrong?'

Mizz Z struggled to sound calmer, to get her thoughts in order. 'When you were coming back to the museum just now,' she asked Jin and Frankie, 'did you see anything in the sky?'

Jin thought hard. 'There was a helicopter,' he said.

'*Ahhh*, yes,' said Mizz Z. 'That was delivering the Crocodile Stones. Without them I couldn't have defeated that cunning old Crocodile King.'

Frankie asked the question she'd almost asked before, at the City Farm. 'Exactly what *are* the Crocodile Stones?'

'I will explain about them later,' Mizz Z told her briskly. 'But apart from the 'copter, what else did you see? You couldn't miss it, this other thing. It filled the sky over the city.'

Frankie and Jin stared at each other and then both slowly shook their heads. 'We didn't see anything,' said Jin.

Mizz Z debated with herself. It was clear to her now that no one else ever saw Darkness. Only the people Avenger hunted down. And they never lived to tell the tale. She was the only person in the world, ever, who had seen Darkness and survived. Should she tell Jin and Frankie about the terrible hound from hell?

No, she decided. *Those kids have been through quite enough already.*

Darkness must stay a secret. Maybe she wouldn't even tell RAAAA. She looked at the whistle, grasped in her trembling fingers. If she blew it, would Darkness come? Or did only Avenger have the power to summon its dog? Mizz Z felt an awful temptation to blow and find out.

Avenger obeyed me, thought Mizz Z. *So maybe Darkness will too.*

She had always been a curious person, ever since she was a little girl. Her fingers were twitching. Power-mad thoughts filled her mind. She lifted the whistle to her lips . . .

'No!' she cried. 'Are you crazy? No more! It is over!' Mizz Z leaped up from the pavement and stood over a drain in the gutter. She opened her hand . . .

Jin rushed over to look down the drain. 'Did you just throw that whistle down there?'

But the whistle had already vanished into the darkness below.

'What did you do that for?' Jin demanded. 'I wanted to keep that.' Then he added,

'There's something you're hiding from us, isn't there? Don't say there isn't, 'cos I can tell.'

Mizz Z should have known she couldn't keep secrets from Jin. But she was saved from answering his questions because right then Dad came striding over. He'd finished his call to the Tangs. 'They're coming down here,' he said, 'as soon as they can.'

'So were they upset about the Iron Dragon?' asked Frankie.

'No, that's the weird thing,' said Dad. 'Once they'd found the rest of the bakery was fine and that the damage would be paid for, I heard cheers in the background. It was almost like they were celebrating. Auntie said, "Freedom at last!" She was already clicking onto the Net, looking for new, modern bun-steaming stoves.'

'Told you,' said Frankie to Mizz Z.

But Mizz Z had suddenly noticed a pink flush in the sky. Surely that couldn't be dawn coming? She checked her watch. 'I must go!' she said.

'I have to meet someone at the airport.'

'I'll drive you,' said Dad.

'No, no,' said Mizz Z, already loping away. 'Thank you. But I will get a taxi.'

Frankie and Jin stared after her, astonished. 'Are you coming back?' called Jin.

Mizz Z stopped and turned round. 'Yes,'she answered. 'I will meet you later. Say around seven this evening. Where will you be?'

Jin wondered, 'What day is it?' He'd lost track of time. Then he remembered: *It's Sunday*. 'Will we be at home?' he asked Dad. They usually were on Sunday night.

To his surprise, Dad was already answering Mizz Z. He was telling her, 'We'll be at City Hall, at the award ceremony. Just say you're my guest. We'll see you there!'

Mizz Z strode away. In the distance, they could hear the wailing of fire engines, heading through the city towards Chinatown.

Frankie turned to Jin, wrinkling her nose. 'Award ceremony? What award ceremony?' she said. 'What's that all about?'

'Dunno. First I've heard of it,' shrugged Jin. 'Hey, Dad, what's this award ceremony?'

But their father was on his mobile again, checking whether the Tangs had left home yet. Frankie shrugged too. 'Well, whatever it is, I won't be there. I'm going to sleep for days.'

Then she stared down into the dark drain. The whistle was probably already on its way out of Chinatown, floating through underground pipes. Soon it would flow into the river, then to the open sea.

'That whistle,' said Frankie, her face screwed up in thought. 'Mizz Z said that after it netted people, Avenger called for something else, something more terrible that scared people to death.'

Jin stared at her, his skin creeping.

'Think it used that whistle to call it?' said Frankie.

'I don't know,' said Jin.

'Wonder what it was,' said his sister. 'The thing more terrible than Avenger.'

'I don't know,' repeated Jin.

There was so much he didn't know. But life was like that with Mizz Z. You just had to accept it. There were always more questions than answers.

Then all thoughts of whistles went right out of his head, because Dad said, 'We've just got time, before Auntie and Uncle turn up, to go get that Giant Pouched Rat.'

'I forgot about him,' said Jin, immediately feeling guilty.

'Well, it's what we came here for in the first place,' said Dad. It seemed to them all like days ago, although it was only a few hours. 'We came to remove a rat from the City Museum. And I don't like leaving a job unfinished.'

'Come on then, let's go,' said Jin.

Dad led the way. 'Stay here and wait for Auntie and Uncle,' he told Frankie over his shoulder. 'They'll be about ten minutes.'

'How do I explain what I'm doing here?' Frankie asked.

'Just be creative,' said Dad.

'You mean *lie*?'

'That's right,' said Dad. 'Think you can do that?'

'Oh, yeah!' grinned Frankie. 'I can do that really well.'

Dr Cramp let Jin and Dad into the museum. The hospital had checked him over and let him go. But the curator still seemed traumatized. His hands were twitching and his eyes were flickering about as if, at any moment, he feared the Crocodile King might invade his brain or Avenger appear round a corner.

'What are you still doing here?' Jin demanded. He was surprised Dr Cramp dare show his face after all the trouble he'd caused.

'Because I've got nowhere else to go,' Dr Cramp confessed. 'This museum is my home. I sleep here at night – I have done for twenty years. Of course, the new director doesn't know about that. You won't tell him, will you?' he begged. His green eyes flickered about again. He couldn't stop shuddering.

'It's OK,' said Dad, trying to reassure him. 'Mizz Z has defeated the Crocodile King. And don't worry – Avenger won't be coming back, either.'

The curator stared at Dad wildly, as if to say, 'I don't believe you!' Then he scurried off into the dark to hide somewhere.

Dad shook his head. 'Poor confused old guy. His mind's completely gone. It's pitiful.'

'*Huh!*' said Jin. 'You're too kind, Dad!' Maybe he would forgive the curator one day for nearly causing the deaths of Frankie and Mizz Z. But he couldn't do it yet – the memories were too raw.

Dad hitched up his rat-fighting belt. 'Come on,' he said. 'Let's go get our rat.'

Jin saw the light of battle in Dad's eyes. He recalled what Dad had said earlier: 'It's me versus the vermin.'

'Hey, Dad,' he said anxiously as he hurried to catch up. 'No rough stuff. This rat is our friend, remember. I want to keep him as a pet.'

As soon as they reached the main hall, Jin

picked up the trail. You didn't have to be a tracking expert to see it. Rat droppings led in a wavy line through the wrecked Toilets of the World exhibition.

'I think he's in there,' whispered Dad, pointing to the small room where the baobab was.

That's weird, thought Jin. When they'd first found him, the Giant Pouched Rat couldn't wait to get out of there. He'd run from that room like a rocket.

But then, for the first time, Jin noticed the changed atmosphere in the museum. There were no scary vibes, no sense of dread or menace at all, as if a wicked spell had been lifted.

'Look at the tree,' he breathed.

They'd all thought the baobab was dead. But now, amazingly, its branches had blossomed. Each twiggy claw ended in a huge purple and white flower, as if the tree were celebrating its freedom, putting out flags because the Crocodile King's spirit had finally left it after so many hundreds of years.

Jin opened the door in the baobab. His quick eyes searched around the public convenience. Then suddenly, behind the hand-wash basin, he spotted the Giant Pouched Rat.

It came bumbling out, not afraid, but just going about its own ratty business. Jin didn't want to lose it again.

'Catch him, Dad!'

Quickly his dad undid the leather pouch on his belt and, with one neat flick of his wrist, threw his rat-catching net. It landed right on top of its target and the rat sat inside, looking dopily out through the mesh, wondering why the sky had fallen down.

Jin rushed to release him. As the rat snuggled into his arms, he said, 'Great shot, Dad.' Then he added something else. It just slipped out somehow. 'That was as good as Avenger.'

Dad said, 'No, it wasn't. No one's as good as Avenger.'

Jin hadn't meant to say it. But since they were talking about Avenger, he suddenly found himself blurting, 'I saw something, Dad. In its eyes.'

Dad said, '"Saw something"? What do you mean?'

Jin hesitated. 'I think it was happy, Dad. It was like it couldn't wait to jump into that furnace. Like it wanted to.'

Jin was used to people thinking his ideas were bizarre, too way out to be believed. So it was a big surprise when Dad said, 'You know, I could have sworn I saw that too.'

'But it was just a machine, wasn't it?' Jin whispered.

Dad shook his head, 'Who knows, son?' The whole of last night had been so bizarre, he was prepared to believe anything. Even that a machine had feelings.

'And why should it look *happy*?' persisted Jin.

'Maybe it thought it was going to beat the Iron Dragon,' Dad suggested. 'I mean, it couldn't have known, could it, that it was going to be completely incinerated?'

He and Jin stared at each other with troubled eyes, as if both of them knew that questions about the deadly tracker would be tormenting their minds for a very long time.

And Jin couldn't say out loud what his super-sharp intuition was telling him. Because this idea was so weird that he barely believed it himself. So he just thought it, privately, inside his head:

Avenger did know. It did know this was its last mission. And it was really happy about that. Because at last it was free. Free from being somebody's personal assassin, free from being made to hunt cursed people down. That's what Avenger wanted all along, Jin was thinking. *Freedom.*

Chapter Sixteen

It was five o'clock on Sunday evening. Jin had slept for eight hours solid. He was in the kitchen with Dad, eating a very late breakfast.

So far both of them had carefully avoided talking about last night. They hadn't once mentioned the Crocodile King or Avenger. It was as if neither of them wanted to be the first to peer again into that pit of horrors. As if they were both desperately trying to pretend that life was back to normal.

'When are Mum and Smiler and Grandma and Grandad coming back from Hong Kong?' asked Jin, feeding slices of mango to the Giant Pouched Rat, who was stuffing them away in its cheeks for later.

'Wednesday,' said Dad.

Good, thought Jin.

When Mum went away he'd cheered, 'Yay! Freedom!' He thought she policed his life far too much. But now he was missing her more than he'd ever imagined. He was fed up with eating fish-finger sandwiches and wearing his least dirty pair of underpants. And with getting into trouble at school for forgetting his tie.

'What is this award thing tonight, anyway?' he asked Dad. 'You haven't told me yet.' He'd already guessed it would be boring. But he was looking forward to going, because Mizz Z would be there.

'It happens every year,' said Dad. 'It's when the council gives out prizes to its best workers.'

'So why didn't I know about this before?' Jin yawned.

'I have mentioned it before,' said Dad. 'But you probably weren't listening. Besides, it's no big deal.'

'If it's no big deal, why do you have to be so smart?' asked Jin.

Dad always wore either his rat-fighting gear, or jeans and a T-shirt. But today he had his best suit on. It was his only suit, which he wore for weddings and funerals, and he looked really uncomfortable in it.

'These trousers have shrunk,' Dad said, trying to suck in his belly. Now he was trying to knot his tie. 'Do you know how to tie ties?' he asked Jin.

'Me?' said Jin. 'No, Mum always does mine.'

That's why, since Mum had been in Hong Kong, he'd been turning up every day at school without it. It was better to lie – 'I've forgotten it' – than have some teacher shout, 'Jin Aaron Sparks, do up that tie!' Then have to struggle with it in front of all the other kids.

He could do it, if he took his time. But not when he was being rushed, with people watching. Then his hands just got more and more clumsy.

'I'm useless at knotting ties,' said Dad.

'Well, I'm dyspraxic,' said Jin, feeding the

rat another mango slice. 'What's your excuse?'

'I'm dyspraxic too,' Dad replied.

Jin stopped feeding the rat. It was as if he'd just jumped into a freezing cold lake. For a few seconds he was in shock – he couldn't breathe, or speak. At first, his mind was numb too. Then it spun through emotions like a fruit machine.

It finally stopped at anger. 'Why didn't you tell me!' he exploded. Furious thoughts raged around his head: *All those times I felt like an alien! Like I was the only dyspraxic one in the whole family!*

Dad looked genuinely puzzled at Jin's reaction. 'I thought you knew.'

'How could I know if no one told me?'

'I thought Mum told you.'

'Well, she didn't!' raved Jin. 'If I'd known I wouldn't have felt so *different*.'

'But didn't you guess?' said Dad. 'What about my tattoos?'

Jin was so surprised that he stopped spluttering with fury. 'What about them?' he asked.

'Well, what do you think they said? Before they got faded?'

'I always thought they said LOVE and HATE.'

'That's what I *tell* everyone,' said Dad. 'But they didn't.'

Jin stared at the blurred letters. Then he had one of his sudden, amazing flashes of inspiration.

'Those letters said LEFT and RIGHT, didn't they?' he said. 'Because you're like me. You can't tell the difference between your right hand and your left.'

Dad grinned. 'Spot on, son. Actually this hand says R-I-T-E because there weren't enough knuckles for R-I-G-H-T.'

And suddenly Jin's anger just fled away, like the Crocodile King out of his mask. He thought about all the little tricks he used to cope with being dyspraxic, such as 'forgetting' his school tie, for instance.

'Nice one, Dad!' he said, exploding this time with laughter. 'I should get tattoos like that.'

'No way!' said Dad, looking seriously afraid he might do it. 'You're not old enough. Your mum would go mental.'

Jin was still grinning when they arrived at the Town Hall. The more he thought about it, the more he marvelled that he hadn't guessed before that Dad was dyspraxic. It seemed so obvious now. Look at all the things he and Dad had in common – like noticing details, for instance, and being extra-alert to atmosphere.

'Which is why we're both good at tracking. *Doh!*' Jin scolded his own daftness. He was so good at reading other people, even strangers. But when it came to his own dad, who he saw every single day, he'd been completely blind.

As Dad parked his yellow council van, Jin said, 'Hey, Dad! This looks like a big do. Mum should be here. She likes a party.'

'She wanted to come,' said Dad. 'But we didn't find out about this until after she'd booked Hong Kong.'

There were crowds of people thronging

into City Hall, all dressed in their poshest clothes. The Lord Mayor had just stepped out of his chauffeured limo, a heavy golden chain dangling round his neck. There was a red carpet on the steps. Even a photographer from the *Newcastle Chronicle*.

'Mr Sparks! Mr Sparks!' he shouted as camera flashes went off, right in Dad's face.

The crush in the lobby was terrible. The noise of chatter was deafening. People were lining up to shake Dad's hand, to slap him on the back.

Jin thought, bewildered, *What's going on?* Now he'd lost sight of Dad. He could feel himself getting hot and flustered. He hated crowds and people pushing and jostling him, invading his space.

Then suddenly a weird thing happened. In his mind, he wasn't in that mob of people any more. He was out on the wide, gleaming, empty river. Just him, floating away on his plastic foam board, surfer dude, riding gentle waves to who knows where. It was so peaceful, with the night sky reflected in the shimmering water. Like he was trailing his fingers through the moon and stars . . .

Someone grasped his arm. 'Jin, are you OK?'

It was Frankie. Suddenly Jin wasn't riding his surfboard. He was back in the City Hall lobby. But he didn't feel like he was losing it any more. Inside, he felt strangely calm and in control. He took a deep breath and told Frankie, in a confident voice, 'Yeah, I'm cool.' Then he said, 'But what are *you* doing here? Thought you were still in bed.'

'My phone woke me up,' said Frankie. 'It was Mizz Z. She told me to come. Actually' – Frankie grinned – 'she said, "Move your bones, girl! Get yourself to the Town Hall!"'

'Sounds like her,' said Jin. 'So where is she, then?'

'Don't know,' said Frankie, staring around. 'She should be here.'

'I bought the Giant Pouched Rat to show her,' said Jin. 'You remember that old cat-carrying case we had? He's in that, out in Dad's van.'

'Think she'll really want to see a *rat*?' said Frankie doubtfully.

The crowd in the lobby was getting thinner. People seemed to be going off somewhere else. And suddenly Jin began to recognize faces. It seemed like almost everyone he knew in his life was here! There was Mr Ma from the grocery, and Auntie and Uncle Tang waving at him.

'Our new bun-steaming stove is on its way!' shouted Auntie. 'Tell Mizz Z thank you. Thank you so much!'

Frankie drifted away somewhere. Jin was standing alone, staring around, when a familiar voice said, 'This is certainly a most glittering occasion.'

Jin spun round. 'Mizz Z!'

She was looking magnificent, in crimson and white with a new matching headwrap to replace the one Avenger had shredded.

'Tonight your dad will get what he deserves,' she said.

'What?' said Jin, looking totally blank.

'Do you not know what is going on here?' asked Mizz Z, gazing down at him from her great height. 'It is in all the papers, on the website of the City Council. It is big news.'

'I don't read the news,' said Jin.

'*Tut, tut*,' said Mizz Z, her eye flashing in disapproval. 'Children should keep themselves well informed. Anyhow,' she added, 'you will soon find out. In the meantime, I want you to meet someone. Here is my little brother, Kapito. I've told you a lot about him – how he escaped from Zilombo's underwater den, for instance.'

A young man appeared from behind Mizz Z and, smiling, shook hands with Jin. 'Pleased to meet you,' he said. Then he melted back into the crowd. 'See you later, sis!'

And suddenly, like a lightning flash, Jin realized something. As usual, he blurted out his thoughts: 'You weren't worried about yourself, were you?' he said to Mizz Z. 'You had to stay alive for Kapito's sake. You had to defeat the Crocodile King and then destroy Avenger, so the curse wouldn't pass on to him?'

Mizz Z's hawk-like features softened. She reached down and placed one hand gently on Jin's head, as if she was giving him her blessing. 'As I believe I said once before,' she told him, 'you are a very wise child, Jin Aaron Sparks.'

Jin's cheeks flushed pink. To change the subject he asked Mizz Z one of the many questions that were troubling him: 'What about the Croc King's spirit?'

'*Shhh*,' said Mizz Z. 'We do not want the whole world knowing RAAAA's business.' She hustled Jin behind a pillar, away from the crowd, before she answered. 'You mean, is his spirit still around?' she said in her usual direct, no-nonsense way. 'It has probably shrivelled up. But even if did survive, with the costume gone and Avenger destroyed, it has lost all its power. It can never become flesh and blood again. Or put curses on people. By the way,' she added, 'please say nothing to Kapito about last night. I don't want him worried.'

'What does Kapito do?' asked Jin. 'Does he work for RAAAA too?'

'No, he has nothing to do with ancient artefacts. He works in America, designing computer games,' Mizz Z said proudly. 'He has his own company. He is very successful.'

'Wow!' said Jin, impressed. 'Did he design *Zombie Dawn*? Because that's my absolute favourite.'

Suddenly a shriek came from somewhere: 'Hey, Jin! I've been looking for you every-where!'

'It's Mum!' said Jin, staring in astonishment. Grandad and Grandma Tang were with her. Grandad was carrying Smiler. 'I thought you weren't coming back from Hong Kong until Wednesday,' he said, rushing over.

'At the last minute I managed to change our plane tickets,' said Mum. 'We came straight from the airport – we didn't want to miss your dad's big night. And I bought you a phone.'

'A phone,' said Jin. 'Cool. Thanks, Mum!'

'It's in my suitcase,' said Mum. 'I'll give it to you later. By the way, did you know you've still got a skull plaster on your face?

Jin reached up to feel. He couldn't believe the plaster was still in place, after all last night's panics: the chase through the alley-ways, almost being netted by Avenger, the rescue on the mud flats, Mizz Z's epic battle with the Crocodile King, the Iron Dragon blowing up . . .

True, the plaster was flapping a bit at one corner.

I'm not going to take it off now, thought Jin, after it had stuck to him through so much. He pressed it firmly down and followed every-one to the award ceremony.

He sat with Mizz Z in the huge hall packed with people. All the seats around him were filled with his friends and family: Mum, Grandad and Grandma Tang, Smiler, Auntie and Uncle Tang and loads of others.

But where was Dad? Jin looked around

but he couldn't see him anywhere. Council employees trooped up to the stage, received an award for their good work and shook hands with the Mayor. Everyone clapped politely.

Jin was just starting to yawn and think, *Why are we here? When is this going to end?* when the Mayor announced, 'And now for the biggest award of the evening! The prestigious "Golden Rat" for our top rodent control technician goes to that legend in rat-catching circles, that superstar of rodent control, Mr Aaron Sparks!'

Dad lumbered shyly up onto the stage, blinking in the flurry of camera flashes. He took his award, a small golden statue of a rat on a pedestal, from His Worship the Mayor.

The whole place went wild. People clapped and whooped. Jin's family raised the roof.

'I never knew Mum could whistle that loud!' Jin exclaimed.

'I never knew our dad was famous,' said Frankie. 'Remind me to show him a lot more respect.'

Mizz Z looked down her nose at Frankie. 'So, does that mean you did not show him respect before?' she asked, raising one eyebrow. Then she added, in a friendly voice, 'I believe I show respect for you, don't I? Perhaps you should show respect for people in your turn. Especially when, like your dad, they deserve it.'

Frankie didn't answer – but she did have the grace to blush. Jin was going to chip in and blurt out, 'Yeah! And Dad's dyspraxic too, did you know that?'

But suddenly that information seemed irrelevant. What difference did it make to anything? They couldn't be cheering Dad any louder if they'd tried. So Jin shut his mouth and stayed quiet, and he and Frankie clapped, bursting with pride, until their hands were sore.

'I think I might have been wrong about Dad,' Frankie admitted to Jin. 'He's not such a loser as I thought.'

Jin smiled. It was the closest Frankie would ever get to apologizing.

At last the applause died away and Dad left the stage. Everyone sat down while the Mayor wound up the award ceremony with a boring final speech.

'*Psst*,' Mizz Z hissed to Jin. 'I almost forgot. Did you re-capture the Giant Pouched Rat?'

'Yes,' said Jin. 'He's in the van outside.'

'Does he have a brown star shape on his throat?'

'Yeah, he does,' nodded Jin, unsure where this was leading.

'Well, the people in my village want him back.'

'What?' said Jin, dismayed. 'I wanted to keep him as a pet. I was going to give him a name.'

'He is nobody's pet,' said Mizz Z. 'And he already has a name. It's Pandu, which means *hero*.'

'You're kidding me!' said Jin, thinking of the sweet-natured, dopey, bunny-like creature. 'Him, a hero?'

'Do not be deceived,' Mizz Z replied.

'Heroes come in many guises. Pandu is a sniffer rat, trained to sniff out land mines. He's worked in war zones all over the world and has saved many lives. He was enjoying a well-earned retirement in my village until, somehow, he got sent over here in the Croc King's spirit tree. Now he needs to go back to Africa, where he belongs. And I must go too.' She checked her watch. 'Right now, in fact.'

'What?' said Frankie, bewildered. 'I thought you were staying for a bit.'

'Unfortunately, no,' said Mizz Z. 'The RAAAA helicopter is picking me up from the museum roof.'

Jin and Frankie stared at each other. At last, the Mayor had finished talking. Chairs were clattering, people were surging past, leaving the hall. Relatives were speaking to them. Auntie said, 'They are serving refreshments on the first floor. Are you coming?' But neither Frankie nor Jin took any notice. At that moment, no one existed for them but Mizz Z.

'I don't understand,' Jin asked her. 'Why all the rush?'

'I am in big trouble at RAAAA,' said Mizz Z. 'They want my immediate report. They may decide I'm no longer fit to be Chief Inspector.'

'Are they crazy? You did a great job!' Frankie protested.

'Well, that is not RAAAA's opinion,' said Mizz Z, tight-lipped.

Jin opened his mouth to add his protests but Mizz Z silenced him with one glance. It seemed she didn't want to discuss it any further.

'Frankie,' she ordered, 'will you find your dad and get the van keys. I will collect Pandu and take him with me.'

Frankie took one look at the Chief Inspector's grim face and instantly obeyed. As she dashed off through the crowd, Jin was left alone for a few moments with Mizz Z.

There was a terrible struggle going on in his mind. He knew Mizz Z blamed herself because ancient artefacts had been destroyed. And RAAAA, too, were obviously really annoyed. Jin wanted to say, 'You did Avenger a favour! It didn't want to go on for ever tracking down cursed people, being someone's professional assassin. You set it free.' But would knowing that make Mizz Z feel better? It might make her feel worse, if she thought Avenger had feelings, wasn't just a machine, and she'd sent it to its death.

And besides, Jin argued with himself, *you don't know for certain.*

Then Frankie came running back with the van keys and Jin still hadn't decided and his chance was gone.

Panting, Frankie told Mizz Z, 'We're coming with you.'

'What, to Africa?' said Mizz Z. 'That is impossible.'

'No, to the museum,' said Frankie. 'To the roof. To see you off. To wish you luck.'

Mizz Z's face softened. 'All right,' she said. 'I would like that. But let's get moving.

The museum is twenty minutes' walk away.'

'No, it's not,' said Frankie. 'I know a short cut. We have to go through a gap in a fence and across some waste ground but we can be there in five minutes.'

'Let us go, then,' said Mizz Z. Head held high, haughty as a queen, looking like she could take on the world, Mizz Z strode out of City Hall onto the streets. Only Jin and Frankie, scurrying after her, knew that her beloved job was on the line. That she might lose everything she'd spent her life working for.

As they reached the City Museum, the sun was setting. They climbed the fire escape up to the roof. Jin carried Pandu, in the cat case.

'Here it comes,' said Mizz Z, pointing to the west. The RAAAA helicopter swooped in from a sky striped with grey and pink. It hovered overhead, whipping up a mini whirlwind, then landed lightly as a bird on the roof.

'Give Pandu to me,' said Mizz Z.

'Aren't you taking Kapito too?' asked Jin.

'No,' laughed Mizz Z. 'Kapito is a big boy now. He has his own life.'

As Jin handed over the case, he took a last look inside. 'Bye, Pandu. You're going back home to Africa.'

The old hero rat, his cheeks stuffed full of mango, was snuggled down in the straw. After being driven out of toilet bowls and crocodile masks, at last he'd found a nice peaceful place to snooze.

Now there was only Mizz Z to say good-bye to.

'Don't look so glum,' she told Jin and Frankie. 'I shall tell you a joke to make you laugh. Do you know the baobab tree?'

Jin and Frankie nodded.

'Well, its other name is the "dead rat tree". That is a very suitable tree for your dad, isn't it?'

Then Mizz Z startled them by throwing back her shoulders and letting out a big, deep belly laugh. Jin didn't have the heart to tell her that Dad had told that joke already. And it wasn't funny then.

'*Teeheehee*,' said Jin politely.

Mizz Z stopped laughing and glared at them with her fierce amber eye. 'Kids in the UK have no sense of humour,' she said, shaking her head sorrowfully. Then she strode, carrying Pandu, towards the helicopter. Just before she got in she turned and waved.

'Will we see you again?' asked Jin.

Mizz Z's face became serious. She gave the brave, defiant tilt of her chin they knew so well. 'I shall not give up my job without a fight,' she told them. 'You can depend on that.' Then she climbed into the 'copter.

'Good luck!' shouted Frankie. But you couldn't hear her above the thudding noise of the rotor blades.

The 'copter lifted from the roof and swooped away across the city, flashing fiery red in the dying rays of the sun.

Sitting inside it, with Pandu in his case beside her, Mizz Z was thinking about the mission that had just ended. Her career might be in ruins, she'd had to destroy the two ancient artefacts she had come to inspect – but she had saved one artefact from the wreckage.

She opened her hand. In her palm lay the whistle that Avenger had used to summon its dog, Darkness. She'd been going to throw it away down the drain. But at the very last second, she just couldn't. She had seen what the whistle could do. She was the only living witness. The only witness, ever.

Such a tiny thing, thought Mizz Z, staring at the delicate bone whistle. Yet it was a thousand times more powerful than the crocodile costume, or even Avenger. Once again, she felt a terrible urge to blow the whistle, to see if Darkness would come at her command. The thought of being in control of such mysterious and deadly ancient forces made even Mizz Z's head swim. With an almost superhuman effort, she resisted.

'No, it wouldn't be right,' she told herself, before adding, 'Except, of course, in the most extreme emergency.'

She closed her hand over the whistle again and settled down for a long flight.

Back on the roof, Jin and Frankie were still staring into the sky, at the spot where they'd last seen the 'copter before it vanished over the horizon.

'I forgot to ask Mizz Z about the Crocodile Stones,' said Frankie. 'Or what happened when Avenger blew that whistle.'

'Ask her when she comes back,' said Jin.

'If she ever comes back,' said Frankie sadly.

They both stared into the sky for a few more minutes, as if they might catch a final glimpse. But the helicopter was far away now, over the North Sea.

'She'll be back,' Jin murmured softly to himself as he gazed up at the stars. 'I *know* she will.'

FOR A PEEK AT JIN AND FRANKIE'S
EXCITING FIRST ADVENTURE WITH MIZZ Z
CARRY ON READING . . .

Chapter One

Madalitso dragged a chair over to her wardrobe. It took almost all her strength. Shakily she climbed up onto it. Her legs were as thin as sticks. But her eyes blazed with fierce determination.

Her lips began to move. 'Are you listening, Zilombo?' she whispered. 'I know you can hear me in there.'

She was talking quietly. There were only two things on top of her wardrobe. One was a battered cardboard suitcase – the one she'd brought with her sixty years ago, when she came to England from Africa. The other was a ball of dried mud, slightly bigger than a football and covered in dust and cobwebs.

'I have kept you shut up here for twenty years,' said Madalitso. 'That is a harsh punishment. But what else could we do after the terrible thing you did?'

Madalitso had a strange expression on her wrinkled face: anger and fear and sorrow all mixed up. She whispered on, wobbling on her chair, 'I want you to know that this afternoon the inspector is coming. Yes, it's that time again! Time for her yearly visit, to make sure you can't escape. But there's no chance of that, is there? Not while I'm still alive.'

Madalitso didn't notice a baby crawl in from the other room. The baby had spiky black hair. His face was shiny with drool.

He smeared the drool off his face with his chubby fist. Then he opened his fingers like a starfish, so the spit stretched between them in glistening strands. His face split into a big gummy grin, pleased at his own cleverness.

The baby looked up. He seemed to see Madalitso for the first time. His eyes grew round with amazement. He held up his slimy hand to show her his drool cat's cradle.

'Goo!' he said.

For years Madalitso had kept her prisoner

secret. And now someone was spying on her! She thought, relieved, *It's only Smiler!*

But now her chair was rocking.

'Aiee!' she cried as she lost her balance. She reached out to grab the wardrobe for support. But that began swaying too. The dried-up mudball rolled to the front of the wardrobe, right onto Madalitso's desperately clutching fingers. She let go. At the same time, the chair slipped from beneath her. Madalitso tumbled to the floor.

A voice yelled from the other room. 'Smiler, are you all right?'

Jin, Smiler's big brother, came bursting into the bedroom. He crashed into the bedside table, spun round and almost trampled Smiler. Then he saw Madalitso, lying curled up, not moving, on the floor, and his mind scrambled immediately.

In a panic, he thought, *What do I do? What do I do?*

Then 'Get Mum!' his brain screamed at him. Mum was Madalitso's friend. She was out in the back yard, emptying the kitchen bin.

'Mum!' bellowed Jin, loud enough for the whole street to hear. Smiler was the world's sunniest, giggliest baby. But now, scared silly by his big brother's panic, he made his mouth into a square red hole. He started shrieking like a car alarm, just to add to the din.

Jin's mum came racing in, still carrying the bin.

Her quick eyes took in the situation. She dropped the bin, rummaged in her pocket for her mobile. She called an ambulance, then went to kneel beside Madalitso.

For years, Madalitso Lungu had been their next-door neighbour. Then she'd got old and frail and moved two streets away to this bungalow. Jin's mum often came round to do her shopping and housework for her. And when he wasn't busy working, Jin's dad came too, to do all her little odd jobs.

Mum knelt by Madalitso, muttering, 'Where's that ambulance?'